SAVING ELVIS

Mary Yancey-Wheat

ISBN-979-8-9880395-1-8

SAVING ELVIS

For Danny, who was the spark.

For Alan, always there.

SAVING ELVIS

1

The stairs. Those familiar, iconic stairs. They looked different now—rich, amber hardwood, polished and immaculate. The thick white carpet was gone, replaced with a narrow blue-and-white stair runner that climbed nimbly up the steps and turned the corner, out of sight. A different portrait was on the mirrored wall to her left. Jenna wondered when that was replaced. Her right hand gingerly brushed the bannister, creamy white and gold, clean and smooth. How many times had it been repainted? Her fingers closed around the railing and she paused, halfway expecting an alarm of some sort to announce her transgression. Above her, the tiny red light of a security camera winked under the chandelier. She glanced through the bannister at the hall table, where fresh flowers sprang from a vase to greet visitors.

Her foot touched the small carpet of the stairs, guiding her on this long-awaited journey of 15 steps. Had she waited for this moment for years? Or merely days? Her mind was still foggy. Above her, at the top of the stairs, was the housekeeper in a crisp white uniform, patiently waiting for her. Jenna wondered how long the wait had been—how long had she been standing there, contemplating placing her toes on the bottom step? An hour? 30 seconds?

Time suddenly had no meaning after what she'd been through.

Carefully, gently, she eased her weight onto the bottom step, again waiting for some alert to the authorities, and security to arrive in a rush to grab her off the step. She absently brushed the bump on her forehead, formed just 36 hours ago. When no obstacle emerged to stop her, she eased her foot up and moved to the second step. There was still tranquility, so she began a slow ascent, now sharply aware that the housekeeper was looking at her strangely. Jenna knew how oddly she was behaving. To an observer who had not been a part of the last four days of her life, she probably looked like she'd never encountered stairs before. In a way, in this deeply personal and emotional moment, she hadn't.

As she passed the portrait, she realized she didn't recognize the person in the frame, but only partially noted it as she reached the top step and was now facing the increasingly bewildered housekeeper. The blue drapes were not at the top of the stairs—instead there was white and gold trimmed wainscoting, matching the bannister. The housekeeper walked around to the right, motioning for her to follow. Jenna's heart lurched, and her stomach turned over. She was vaguely aware of another security camera in the upper corner, looking down at her. Could it see how nervous she was? She followed the stair rail around the graceful curve, glimpsing only for a second the stained glass that adorned the front door she had just passed through. How was this real? Surely she would wake up now and find the last four days had been a long, complicated dream. Surely. This couldn't actually be happening, could it? It was all so surreal, it made her question, for just a second, as she approached the next door, if this was happening at all. Maybe she was lying somewhere with a head injury and this was a hallucination. Or was she in a hospital somewhere, engulfed in the flames of a high fever, dreaming this as doctors tried to cool her body? She fidgeted with the small silver owl ring on her right hand. It wasn't possible she'd only owned it a few days, was it? To her finger and her heart, if felt as though it had been on her hand for all of eternity.

The housekeeper paused at a white interior door, with a hint of gold trim, and smiled as she indicated this was her destination. Her black flats clicked on the shiny hardwood as she gestured for Jenna to go on in. It occurred to Jenna that the hallway was clean, and light; gone were the opulent trappings of the 60s and 70s. The over-the-top décor and impossibly thick carpeting, once a symbol of style and money, had now long been abandoned for cleaner, more modern tastes.

Slightly to her left a door was ajar, and she knew instinctively that he was behind that door. She stopped, twisted her ring again, and felt her heartbeat quicken. A fast glance to her right found a white door, closed. She turned back to the door at hand and lightly knocked. A quiet male voice responded, but she couldn't make out words. She hesitated, then gently, carefully, pushed the door further open, then peered into what was clearly an office. Open blinds let in light, and a smart, black minimalistic desk was slightly to her right. There was a lovely gray tile floor, and across the room was a well-worn brown leather couch. Jenna froze. The white-haired, elderly man gazed across the office from his place on the couch, motionless. She stepped all the way into the room and stood still, fully facing the man. He wore a crisp white shirt and navy pants—classic, subdued, stylish. Silence stretched between them as he took her in through tinted glasses. He did not move, he did not speak.

Jenna smiled a small smile and said, "As promised, here I am." She held her palms up and shrugged slightly.

Still the man didn't move. Did he remember her at all? Had the years stolen from him who she was? What they had shared and accomplished? Was his mind and memory intact? A rush of panic fluttered through her.

The man slowly reached up and removed his glasses. His hands, though older and more arthritic than she remembered, were the familiar hands she knew. She looked at his now bare face. The blue eyes, now paler with time, were the same eyes she expected. They took her in, slowly and deliberately, and a smile spread across his so-familiar face. He held out his hands to her.

"Jenna, you came!" The voice, unchanged, caused her eyes to sting with tears of affection.

"Elvis!" she said as she raced to him and sat by him on the couch. "Of course I came! I promised, didn't I?"

He smiled and pulled her to him in an embrace. She hugged him tightly, taking in his familiar feel and scent. He still smelled like wisps of Old Spice and cigars.

"I've missed you. Not a day has passed when I haven't thought of you, hoping you'd come like we planned," he said, his voice thick with emotion.

"I got here as quick as I could," she said, noting he was thinner.

She pulled back and took his hands again. "Let me see you." She studied him for a moment, realizing the whole plan had worked. The whole long, tedious, wonderful plan had done exactly what it was supposed to do. Slightly thinner, white hair covered his head now, and time had etched lines and wrinkles where there were none the last time she saw him.

"Did you look?" he asked "At Google? Did you see?" He sounded pleased and excited, his smile filled with pride.

"Some, yes. After I got back, I slept for a whole day, then I spent yesterday looking it all up. You've been busy!"

Elvis chuckled. "Yeah, I did the best I could with the information you left me."

"There was so much to take in. The stuff I thought I knew—the things that had always been... Much has changed. I haven't taken it all in yet." Jenna paused, searching his face. "I saw about the miscarriage. I'm so sorry."

A look of discomfort crossed his face and his eyes clouded. "Thanks. That was a difficult time—we were heartbroken. So long ago…" He trailed off and looked down.

"Three days…" Jenna laughed. They embraced again and she stood up, looking around. "Boy, this place has changed, hasn't it?"

Elvis stood up, much more steadily than she expected. He reached for a gold cane and leaned on it slightly.

"It's not a memorial to a dead man now." He beamed. "A lot of changes were made in a very short period of time."

"I can see!" Jenna exclaimed, looking around again. "Man, when you decide to do something, you go all out!"

He laughed, and Jenna thought he might have the best laugh in the world. She was so glad that hadn't changed.

Just then the front door banged and a female voice called "Dad?" up the stairs. Jenna's heart jumped. Lisa was here. She had no idea what he had shared with his daughter as she grew up. Did she know any of this crazy story? As the footsteps on the stairs grew closer, Jenna felt an almost overwhelming urge to run away and go home, to not meet this adult daughter of this man who had become so important to her. What if she didn't approve of Jenna? What if she didn't want her near her dad? Jenna was the interloper here. She wanted to flee.

With his ever-present ability to read others, Elvis took her hand and squeezed. "She knows about you.

You're who she came to see." Somehow that made Jenna more skittish.

The office door opened all the way, and there stood a striking, beautiful woman in her 50s. Her long hair was pulled back into a ponytail that trailed down her back, and her black jacket was fit and elegant. Her blue eyes moved from her father to Jenna. She smiled warmly as she strode to Jenna, extending her hand.

"So, here's the famous Jenna. Boy, am I glad to finally see you ag— Umm, meet you. I'm glad to finally meet you. I'm Lisa."

As they shook hands, Jenna noticed an odd exchange between Lisa and her father. They exchanged glances, and Elvis seemed, for a split second, to be shaking his head at her. Lisa stepped over to her father and kissed him. Jenna, for barely an instant, saw Lisa, much younger, with long, loose, blonder hair, curled up on the couch in this room, reading a book. Like a wisp of smoke, the image was gone. She stared at the place on the couch blankly. She shook her head a little and saw Lisa, paused, watching her closely. Elvis cleared his throat.

"Where's Mom?" he asked.

"Still at home," Lisa answered as she leaned around him to set her handbag on the couch. Jenna frantically searched her mind for new information on where "home" was for Elvis' ex-wife—Lisa's mom. She'd seen something about it yesterday as she dug through the internet, taking in the staggering changes she had caused. She remembered the story that Elvis and Priscilla had reconciled for a time, which had resulted in another pregnancy. A miscarriage had followed, and there were further details about the ensuing divorce, but she couldn't remember the specifics.

"I would imagine this is quite a reunion for you two," Lisa said as she settled herself into a black leather chair opposite the couch.

Elvis and Jenna sat on the couch, and Elvis reached for Jenna's hand again. "It's been so long," he said to Lisa, his voice cracking. "I thought a few times we'd never have this reunion. That she'd never know how all this turned out. That something terrible had happened, like she didn't make it back properly, or that she didn't remember…everything. At one point, I was so worried about it I drove to St. Louis to verify she'd been born." He reached over to the small glass coffee table and grabbed his glasses. He put them back on and grinned. "Any memory of a long back limo driving near your house?" He smiled and chuckled.

"No, but I wouldn't have known to be looking for one!" said Jenna. Her smile flickered as a fleeting image of herself getting into the back of a black limousine flashed through her head like lightening and then was gone. Jenna had never been in a limo in her life. Had she? What was happening here?

"I knew I shouldn't look, but I was desperate to know you'd been born." Elvis peered at Jenna, as though he expected a reaction.

He looked at Lisa. "So?"

Lisa laughed a hearty laugh. "I've never been so anxious to see another person in my life."

"I was so nervous coming here I nearly threw up," said Jenna. "I know there are so, *so* many changes I just haven't seen yet."

"I bet there are," said Lisa, looking at her dad with deep affection. "He's still here, for one. He told me a little when I was a teenager, but I didn't get more of the story till I was well into my 20s." She paused, looking mischievous. "He also told me what a complete ass he was to you that first day. How he couldn't get his head around it and almost flat-out accused you of kidnapping him to have his baby or something!"

They all laughed and Elvis blushed.

"Yeah he definitely was an ass," Jenna said, leaning back into the couch, finally a little more comfortable. "But anyone would be... Having experienced it myself—it is *so* disorienting."

"He also told me what was changed. What his original...fate had been. I can't even imagine... It's so..." Lisa stopped and looked at her dad for a moment, clearly needing a second. "Okay, then. I am here for the duration," Lisa said, clearing her throat. "Dad always told me that on or around this day in 2022, I'd hear it all. So here I am."

"God, where to even begin?" Elvis said.

"At the beginning?" asked Jenna, laughing.

"Let's go downstairs to the den and get really comfortable. We can have some iced tea and sandwiches or something," said Lisa, standing up.

Just as they rose to collect themselves, a cell phone began to audibly vibrate. Elvis pulled an iPhone from his pants pocket and tapped it to answer.

"Hi! Yeah, she's here. Lisa got here a while ago. Oh, now? Okay, hang on." He held the phone away from him and tapped, and Jenna heard the familiar facetime ring. It was immediately answered by a female voice. Elvis turned the screen around to face Jenna and there she saw Priscilla on the screen.

"Hello!" she said. "I'm so very sorry I'm missing this meeting! There's an opening of one of the Presley charity events here in LA and I have to be here. I hope we can meet in person very soon! Our whole family owes you a great deal."

"It's all right, I understand. I hope we can meet as well!" Jenna stammered. It was a consistent surprise, the people she kept meeting. It occurred to Jenna that it seemed strange to hear gratitude regarding her adventure with Elvis. Of course she'd done it. She couldn't imagine having said no.

Elvis turned the phone around and smiled at the screen. "We're heading downstairs. I'll call you later." He turned the phone toward Lisa, who called "Love you!" over her shoulder as she headed for the hallway. The call ended and they moved to the stairs. Elvis was amazingly nimble for 87 years old, and much more solid on his feet than Jenna would ever have expected.

When she had awakened from her 12-hour sleep, she anxiously scoured the internet for hours, seeking the changes, details, and stories the last five days had created. There had been so much…just *so* much.

Elvis' had been a life well-lived after they had said their goodbyes that day in Vegas. The whole decade of the 1970s had been entirely different than her prior knowledge of his career. Gone were the bejeweled capes and flashy jumpsuits, replaced with more suits, jumpsuits that were less flamboyant and quieter, sophisticated two piece ensembles. The wild spending sprees were absent from the articles of the day, as was his apparent descent into depression. In its place were hundreds—no, thousands—of stories and photos of a dynamic, successful career from a reasonably healthy, vibrant man. Songs formerly connected to other artists now bore "Elvis Presley" as the performer. He had cowritten many songs, as well as performed them. There were dozens more chart-topping albums, and world tours had included Asia, Europe, Australia, and New Zealand.

The 1980s had shown a slight decrease in live performances and concerts, and she ran across an article from 1984 indicating Elvis had undergone a surgical procedure and had taken a few months off in the summer. In 1985 he played a concert in London for the Queen, 22 years after the original invitation. He had recorded new and old songs with the Philharmonic. He had done several more TV specials, all to critical acclaim.

She found articles about his separation from Priscilla, their reconciliation in 1973, and the miscarriage of a pregnancy. They had officially divorced in 1975. That story caused Jenna to wince. She knew that the loss of a second child and the end of his marriage had hit him hard. The subsequent stories and photos about how close he had remained to Priscilla helped, but she knew this must have been a terrible time for Elvis.

There were several articles about Elvis' father, Vernon, passing away in 1990 at the age of 74. She smiled at the photos of a 55 year old Elvis at his father's funeral with Priscilla and Lisa, who was now 22. Elvis looked so stately, so self assured. Though she saw grief on his face and sadness in his eyes, she also saw a man at peace with himself. Inky, jet black hair, now relegated to a thing of the 60s, had long changed over to a dark brown, more in keeping with his natural color. She chuckled to herself when she saw his trimmed down sideburns.

His charity work was at the forefront of every search. He had established foundations all over the world, providing funding for everything from clean water and schools in Africa to job skills and training in the U.S. He raised money, gave away scholarships, and was involved in housing through Habitat for Humanity as well as several other foundations he had established. The Presley charities, run by Priscilla and Lisa, were vast and varied, and had lifted millions out of poverty and improved lives in countless ways.

The one overriding thing Jenna noted was the absence of the Colonel. She had found an article that they had parted ways in 1973, after his famous *"Aloha From Hawaii"* concert. His first world tour appeared to begin in late 1973 and continued into 1974. She found one article titled "Elvis seeks new management," but no amount of scrolling produced much information. Jenna wondered why.

The last 23 years since 2000 had shown two more Vegas residencies and multiple collaborations, with everyone from Elton John to Celine Dion. Jenna had clicked several videos of these duets and was moved. His voice hadn't changed much at all. He sounded as rich and beautiful as he had the last time she saw him. He had established a huge social media presence, and was quite regular with posts. He had millions of followers. There were also multiple pictures of him with a younger woman, but her face never really showed in the pics. Goodness, the back of her head sure resembled Jenna's. She wondered who that was.

At the bottom of the stairs, Jenna looked to her right and noticed the marble floor in the dining room had not been altered, nor had the overall color scheme. The curtains looked different, but she couldn't place how as they turned to head through the kitchen toward the den. She had the strangest sense of déjà vu as they moved through the house. The kitchen was a completely different space—it was utterly transformed with all white and black tile, black cabinets, and stainless steel appliances. Jenna paused for a second, staring at an upper cabinet. For a moment, she was absolutely certain she knew what was in that cabinet—she even had a flash in her head of opening it and reaching into it. She absolutely *knew* there were coffee cups behind that glossy black door. How could that be? She shook her head. That couldn't be. Elvis continued down the steps into the den, and Jenna was so preoccupied with trying to remember something about that cabinet that she didn't notice him watching her intently, almost expectantly. Security cameras were monitored on the six small screens in a row on the far side of the kitchen, and Jenna saw the three of them on the left monitor as they passed into the den.

"Wow!" Jenna said, stopping short. "*This* is different." Where she expected to see the famed Jungle Room, she saw dark wood laminate floors, cozy black and beige sectionals, and welcoming armchairs. A large, flat-screen TV was on the now-white wall where the waterfall had been, and stylish abstract area rugs had replaced the infamous green carpeting. She looked up and saw there were sound tiles on the ceiling, so she knew he recorded here.

"The Jungle Room sure has been updated!" Jenna exclaimed. Lisa paused and looked at her strangely.

"What? The what?" she asked, puzzled.

"Never mind." Jenna blushed. Elvis grinned. Lisa stepped back into the kitchen to speak to the cook about sandwiches and refreshments, and Jenna and Elvis made their way to the comfortable couches. Jenna sat in an armchair next to the edge of the couch where Elvis settled. He set his cane against the glass coffee table and angled himself toward Jenna. He smiled warmly and extended his left hand. Jenna took it and gently squeezed the thin hand. Arthritis poked her from slightly swollen knuckles.

"I can't tell you how happy I am! Your whole life changed. It seems like everything is different!"

Elvis nodded. "It's been so long… But man, I remember everything we agreed on before you left. I held tight to the ideas and basic plan. I had to."

Jenna saw dozens of framed gold records and awards adorning the wall across from her. He'd gotten so much more living done! Elvis looked proudly at Jenna.

"These are some of my favorites, so I keep them here," he said.

Lisa returned, and instead of sitting on the couch by her father, she dragged another armchair to the edge of the coffee table to Jenna's left.

"Lorraine will bring our refreshments in a while." She smiled at her dad, then turned to Jenna.

"Okay, here we are. Tell it. Tell it all."

Jenna was nervous. Where to even begin? How does one impart a tale that is so outlandish, so unbelievably ridiculous, in a way that will sound even remotely credible?

Elvis set his cell phone on the table and crossed his legs, releasing her hand. Lisa leaned back slightly and adjusted her weight. Jenna breathed deeply and closed her eyes for a moment before she began.

2

Jenna pulled into her usual parking space on campus, blaring Suspicious Minds, readying herself for the meeting with her boss. She was taking four weeks off from the university to attend to her grandmother's estate and post-funeral paperwork, and to get some much-needed rest. Jenna was burned out, grieving her Nan's passing, and in desperate need of a break. She decided to take the rest of March off to recoup and get herself back together. It had been a long winter.

She put the Jeep into park and shut off the engine. As she opened the door, her peripheral vision caught a glimpse of movement near a stand of small trees, but when she turned to look, she saw nothing. She pulled her bag onto her shoulder, looked back at her Jeep, and started to walk in. She cast a mental post-it note into her brain that she needed a new "I ♥ Elvis" sticker for her back window.

A chilly breeze grabbed at her legs as she pulled the door to the building open and stepped inside. The door clicked shut behind her, and she looked back toward her car again, sensing she was being watched. A man was standing near her car, looking at the door she has just entered. Was this the same man she'd seen yesterday as she was leaving the funeral home? Or three days ago at the florist? Now that she thought about it, was this the same man she saw near her bank over a week ago? And even longer ago when she was pumping gas? Surely she was being paranoid and ridiculous. Surely. No one would be following her.

Dr. Kaplan, Jenna's immediate supervisor, was standing at the window as she entered his office. He seemed to be looking at something specific, and his face was focused and concentrated.

"Al?" she asked, stepping into his office.

"Oh, Jenna, yes. Come in," he answered absently, only glancing at her before turning back to the window. Jenna sat on the couch across from his desk, and when he didn't say anything, she ventured a small cough.

He turned and motioned for her to come over to the window.

"Look," he said, pointing down at Jenna's car. "Do you know those two?"

Jenna shook her head as she looked past Al's shoulder at her car. There were two men in dark blazers and light shirts, trying to look as though they *weren't* near her car. Al turned and sat down at his desk, and Jenna looked back to the window. She clearly saw one man with dark hair muttering into a device that looked like a cell phone, then, after nodding to his colleague, he literally vanished into thin air. He actually faded into nothing right in front of her eyes. Jenna made a small strangled noise in her throat as her eyes showed her something her brain refused to process. She turned around and looked at Al, who looked up and said, "What?"

"Did…that guy…just…" she started. Al looked concerned and rose to join her at the window again. They watched the man with light hair get into a small, black, nondescript car and drive away. They turned and sat, he at his desk and she on his office couch. After a moment, he said, "Did he what?" His dark brown eyes were baffled.

"I…he… He just…vanished. Into thin air," Jenna said, staring at Al. What in the *world* just happened? After another moment of silence, Al spoke.

"He…disappeared. What do you mean?"

"I mean, he was standing there, and then he wasn't. Like, *poof*. He literally disappeared."

Al looked closely at Jenna. "Hmmm. Well, I'll say this: he looked like the same man who was downstairs about a week ago asking about you. Whether or not he 'vanished' is debatable—he probably just got in the car, but…"

"Umm, no, he vanished. I'm tired but I'm not hallucinating. I saw it." Jenna needed to shift her brain into function again. "Wait. Asking about me? Asking what?"

"The kinds of things a private detective would ask. How long you'd been here, what exactly was your position, who were your colleagues?" Al ran a hand through his wavy salt-and-pepper hair and sighed. "I happened to be down there on another matter and I heard him asking. I went in there and requested ID. He declined and left. I must say it gave me a strange feeling. I wanted to let you know but you had the funeral and so much else going on that I decided to wait and see if he surfaced again."

Jenna nodded. "Well, it seems he did. Who *are* they?"

Shrugging, Al said, "I have no idea. There have been no official requests for information put in to human resources that I do know. So, whatever they wanted was more…informal."

"Why on earth would anyone be asking questions about *me*?"

"I can't imagine. But you're about to go out on leave, so for that month I'd encourage you to be aware of your surroundings. Can you think of any reason why someone might want to be tailing you?"

"No, I can't," Jenna said, feeling a little alarmed. What did these two want? Who were they?

"I'm approving your leave for four weeks. Make sure the teaching assistant has your scheduled plans and lessons. And Jenna, be careful," Al said, looking intensely at her.

"I will," Jenna said as she rose to leave, handing him the leave of absence form she'd filled out earlier. As she left, she chuckled at herself. No one would follow Jenna Logan, of all people. This whole exercise in paranoia was silly. And that man didn't *really* disappear.…

The drive back to her apartment in Germantown was uneventful. Jenna was tired and it was beginning to mist a cold, damp, fog-like rain. This was a day to stay home. She almost ached with fatigue. Her eyes kept glancing into her mirror, scanning for the black car following her. She saw nothing.

She pulled off her shoes and sat on the window bench in her living room, leaning back on her Elvis pillow. She covered herself with a throw and gazed blankly out the window, two stories down, at the mostly empty parking lot. There was a small, featureless black car parked slightly sideways. Was this the car the man had driven off in on campus? How could she know, since a million other cars looked just like it? Two of her neighbors drove cars that were nearly identical.

As she mulled this over, there was a quiet knock at the door. Startled out of her mental search for black car sightings, she felt immediately on edge. She walked to the door. "Who is it?"

"Agents Patterson and James, ma'am," came a male voice. She looked into her peephole and saw some sort of badge already displayed, the gold color winking in the gray rainy light. What on earth was this?

She opened the door a crack and looked warily out at the men standing there. She realized now that she had been followed for days by these men. She felt panic rise as her mind ticked off each time in the last ten days she thought maybe she saw these two and her heart quickened. There were many sightings. Jenna was taken aback at the blinders grief and exhaustion had placed around her normally observant eyes.

"What do you want?"

"To speak with you, ma'am. You're Jenna Logan?" one of them said. They both had on black pants and black blazers. Bland, cream colored shirts and ties seemed to make up some sort of...uniform? Who were these people?

"About what?" she asked.

"Ma'am, it's very complicated. We'll need to explain. Can we please come in? We're federal agents and mean you absolutely no harm," said the taller one with sandy hair. Jenna wondered if Ted Bundy had ever said that.

"Look, I don't know you and..."

"We're aware of how you might be suspicious. There is an explanation, I assure you. We have identification and are unarmed. Please allow us to speak to you," said the shorter one with dark hair. "I'm Bill James and this is Chris Patterson. Please. This is of the highest importance."

Jenna closed the door and stared at the knob. Dare she let them in? What did they want? This could go sideways very quickly. What would federal agents want with a part-time adjunct college professor? She only taught one class this year, and it wasn't exactly about nuclear science.

She hesitated another moment, grabbed the knob, pulled her hand back, then grabbed it again. She gingerly opened the door and stepped back.

The two men slowly stepped over the threshold and delicately closed the door. "Thank you," said the dark-haired one, who identified himself as Bill. "We really appreciate this. We have..." he glanced at his partner "…business to discuss." They exchanged unreadable looks and looked back at Jenna.

"Please, sit down," she said, feebly motioning to the couch and chairs behind her. They moved carefully over to the living room and stood, facing each other, unsure of the next move. Jenna turned and said "I'll put on some tea—make yourselves comfortable."

She stepped around the breakfast bar and into the kitchen. As she filled the copper kettle at the sink, she saw the men perch awkwardly on the two chairs, seeming to avoid the couch. Jenna turned on the burner and returned to her visitors. She sat on the couch, realizing her throw blanket was still around her shoulders. She looked dreadful, she knew. God, she was tired.

"What can I help you with?"

The two exchanged almost grim-looking expressions, and Bill leaned slightly forward. "We need your help," he said, eyes fixed on hers. His long, slim face was set, his eyes keenly focused on her, his body taut and anticipatory. The sandy-haired man with the rounder, softer face was looking alternately from Jenna to Bill. She assessed that Bill was in charge here.

"What can federal agents—or whatever you are—possibly want with me?"

"We *are* federal agents, in a way." Bill looked away from Jenna to Chris.

"In a way? What does that mean?" Jenna was feeling uneasy.

"We are assigned to a department that only...sort of exists," said Chris.

Jenna stared a moment, blinked, then rolled her eyes and sighed. "So I have Austin Powers times two coming to see me. Super." What on earth did these two think? Did they know how ridiculous this was starting to sound?

Bill looked very uncomfortable. "Um, more like...*Men In Black*," he said.

"Ooohhhh. Okay. Got it," said Jenna, pushing off her throw and standing up. "Are we done here? I have stuff to do." She put her hands on her hips.

Bill rose and faced her. "No, wait. Please, hear us out. We've been sent to secure your help—at least please listen."

Jenna considered. What was the worst-case scenario here? *They're two escapees from somewhere and they think they're federal agents?* She looked them both up and down, trying to assess their potential for violence. She scanned their jackets for gun bulges, but saw none.

The kettle's first whistles of warning pulled her from her thoughts and she went back to the kitchen. She prepared the tea, set out chocolate cookies with three cups and carried the heavy tray to the coffee table.

"Sugar? Milk?" she asked as she retrieved three spoons.

"Just sugar is fine. Don't go to any trouble," said Bill.

Jenna reached through the breakfast bar, grabbed the sugar bowl, then returned to her place on the couch as Bill and Chris sat back down. She poured the tea into the cups, aware she was being studied. She pushed the cups and a spoon at each man, then pulled a cup toward herself. She settled back a bit and stirred her tea, looking at them skeptically.

"All right, fine. I'll give you ten minutes to hear what you came to say. When you've finished, you can leave."

"Deal. Thank you," said Bill. He stirred some sugar into his tea, and seemed to be searching for the right opening.

"The agency department we work for falls under several...areas." He didn't look at her, but focused on the cup, continuing to stir. "We... That is...we...understand how outlandish that sounds."

Jenna sipped her tea wordlessly, nodding slightly.

"One of the things that has been under development, originally for wartime use, is a... Well, a time machine. We've mastered time travel."

Jenna smiled. "*Have* you, now?" She nodded again. "Go on." Great. She had two certifiable loons in her living room.

"Yes. It's been in development for about 20 years, but only within the last 3 to 5 years have we been able to develop a finished prototype that works."

"Ah. Uh-huh. Go on"

"So, over the last 18 months a plan to...to... Well, fix the world, in a sense, has come into focus."

Jenna nodded again, wondering if her face was betraying her increasing desire for them to leave. She did not have the patience for this.

Chris scooted forward to the edge of the chair, hands clasped, looking at Jenna imploringly. "As we searched not only the physical mechanics of how this works, we also began to collaborate on what we could use it for, outside of wartime situations, that would benefit, at least on some level, everyone. What if we knew we had the ability to transport a person to another time—would we do it? Where? When? As you can imagine, the possibilities are mind-boggling."

"Certainly," Jenna agreed, sipping her tea to conceal another eye roll.

Bill continued, "We considered dozens and dozens of influential, important figures: Churchill, JFK, MLK, Lincoln, even Patton and MacArthur. We looked at every leader we could think of. Princess Diana was strongly considered. What we need is a universal, across-the-board, unifying force. And then it hit us: we shouldn't be looking at political and world leaders. They're too polarizing. We need an entertainer, someone beloved the world over. We need to save Elvis."

Jenna nearly spit out her tea. She coughed and reached for a napkin. "Elvis," she said into the napkin, half choking, half laughing. "Okay. Sure."

"We're serious. He's the best bet for providing a low-key, unifying force that people from all walks of life not only have in common, but can rally around. Who or what else can you think of that exists *right now* with those qualities?"

Jenna thought. Actually, she had no answer. There was nothing that leapt to mind with universal appeal that far reaching. She gave a little shrug. "So what do I have to do with all this?"

"You're the one we chose to save him," said Bill, watching her intently.

Jenna paused and let out a snorted sort of laugh, and set down her cup. "Uh-huh. Okay."

"We are absolutely serious, Ms. Logan. The class that you teach on the greatest influences of the 20th century? Perfect. You live in Memphis. You teach in Memphis. You know as much about the man as it's possible to know, given that he died eight years before you were born."

Jenna put her hands up, starting to get seriously annoyed at whatever prank these two were playing. "All right, look. Yes, I teach that class. Only a portion of it is about Elvis, though. Yes, I'm a huge fan. Fine. You got me on that. The rest of this... What*ever* this is..." She shook her head and stood up. "Is just...no. I need you both to leave. I don't know what you're doing or who put you up to this, but I have just lost my grandmother and I'm exhausted and I don't have the patience for this." She began walking toward the door to show them out. "*Super* that you stopped by and all, but we're done here." She reached for the doorknob.

"But you're on leave now! This is the perfect time!" said Chris, a sense of pleading in his voice.

Jenna froze, then turned slowly to face them. "How could you *possibly* know about that? That was only a few hours ago!" Her eyes were brilliant blue, fixed on their faces. Who had told them? How could they know about this? Had it been one of them she thought she saw on campus earlier? At the florist? Same guys? Oh, jeez, who actually were these men?

"We were there when Dr. Kaplan turned in the approved request. Well, *I* was. Did we or did we not just explain that we have perfected a time machine?" Bill explained, as though to a child.

Jenna began shaking her head. "No," she said as she went into the kitchen. "No, no, no. This isn't a thing. No." She needed them to leave. *Now.*

Chris began to speak, but Bill cut him off and stepped forward toward the breakfast counter. Now his demeanor had shifted to careful, slow movements, like he feared spooking a scared animal. Jenna felt like a scared animal. One trapped in her apartment with two crazy men. Oh my gawd, she though wildly, they're human traffickers and they're here to force me into a van. She backed up against her sink, wondering if a kitchen knife would suffice in a desperate attempt to save herself.

Bill, seeing actual fear plainly on her face, stepped back and went back to his chair. He motioned to Chris and they both sat back down. "Ms. Logan, we do not intend to harm you. We have simply been sent to secure your participation."

Jenna craned her neck to see over the counter and she saw that they were seated, without apparent weapons. Her heart rate began to return to normal as she cautiously stepped back into the living room. She eased herself over to the couch, carefully not turning her back on them.

"I told you when we arrived, we are not armed. We have no ill intent," Bill said, leaning forward for a cookie. He bit a mouthful and waited.

Jenna breathed deeply. "Okay. Say all this is true. Why me? There are thousands more informed about his life than I am."

"Because of what we said before," said Chris, also helping himself to a cookie. "You're a huge fan. You're so knowledgeable that you teach a college level course around him, and you're close to the age he was when we're planning this, so you'd be a peer. It's also well known that he responded more genuinely and openly to women than he did to men. And, as is human nature, sometimes it's easier to open up and share with a stranger. Someone not familiar to us. If you were part of his inner circle, he would probably be more resistant to hearing this stuff from you. As a matter of fact, he would more than likely outright reject *any* intervention from anyone close to him."

Jenna mulled this over. They were correct in these things, but much of this was also fairly common knowledge. She chewed a cookie and thought. If this was true (How *could* it be?), the preconceived "roles" Elvis was said to have assigned to romantic interests wouldn't apply to her.

"What makes you think he'll listen to anything I say? He doesn't know me from Adam."

"Well, honestly, he'll have just landed in 2022 from 1969. He'll probably have to at least recognize that you aren't just some ardent fan who wants to hold him hostage or something. The physical experience of jumping here will go a long way toward making anything you say legitimate. Trust me, that experience will *definitely* stick with him. That's the plan, by the way—to bring him here."

"From '69," said Jenna flatly. "Why then?"

"Because he was still physically fit and well. Waiting much longer might actually harm him, because his overall health was starting to fail. Earlier than '69, he was unhappy and wanting out of the movie contracts. The peak of his professional and personal contentment is 1969. In our time, we have tools here and now that people close to him then didn't have, like the final result of his choices. We have pictures and videos and autopsy reports. They're going to be hard to deny. He'll have just been whipped through time, flung down into a different year and faced with a complete stranger who knows an insane amount about him and has photographic and video proof."

"Ah. Okay, then." Jenna gazed out the window at the cold, gray day. "I'll admit the logic is reasonable. But please know—I don't for one *second* believe you have a time machine." Her eyes flashed as though she dared them to prove her wrong.

"We thought you'd probably need solid proof. We can provide that for you," said Bill, pulling out a cellphone–sized device from his pocket. He entered a password and it beeped, then fell silent. Jenna gazed at the device. That was the same device she'd seen on the parking lot earlier when he had vanished into thin air.

"Please, if you would, stand over there." He motioned to the open area in front of the door.

She walked over and stood, hands on her hips.

"Do you give me permission to demonstrate this tool?" Jenna spread her arms in an irritated fashion and nodded. "Okay, *proof* incoming. Here you go! See you in a few minutes!"

Jenna watched as he entered something into the device. She felt a slight tingle on her right ankle, and for a minute it seemed as though Chris and Bill were standing in a spotlight as all the other light faded around them. The tingle exploded up her body and engulfed her in a terrifying combination of pins-and-needles sensation and spinning. She felt something or someone shove her roughly, very hard, from behind, and she staggered forward. She tried to put her arms out to catch herself, but they wouldn't move. The prickly, pins-and-needles feeling increased until she thought she would scream, when suddenly she landed on a hard surface, her full weight on her right shoulder. She grunted out loud and rolled into a hard object, then lay still. The tingling had stopped. She opened her eyes. No spinning. As her brain began to process where she was, she sat up with a grunt and massaged her shoulder. Her stomach lurched, and she was dizzy again for a moment.

"God *damn*," she muttered as she looked around. The surface she'd landed on was a worn gray linoleum floor. She had rolled backward into a dirty porcelain sink. The room she was in was small and very dimly lit and smelled like bleach. She saw shelving, mops, buckets. Somewhere in the distance there was a lot of noise. A crowd of people, maybe? A large gathering?

Jenna got up carefully and slowly, holding her shoulder and cursing to herself. She staggered sideways and grabbed the sink as she tried to regain her balance. When she felt steady on her feet, she looked around more closely, realizing she was in a janitor's closet. The narrow door was about 10 feet in front of her, so she went over and cautiously opened it a few inches, leaning on the doorknob for extra support against the lingering sensation that the floor was moving underneath her. The sound of a crowd of people grew louder as the door opened.

She stepped into a hallway, and to her left was an intersection of halls. She could hear the crowd noise coming from the hallway that led to the right from that intersection of halls. She carefully edged around the corner, following the sound of people more than anything else. Where was she? Her fleece slippers were scuffing on the floor, and she realized she was breathing much too loudly.

The hallway led her to a small alcove, which was also dimly lit. As she entered the alcove she heard the crowd of people very loudly to her left. There was clapping, cheering, and screaming. And music. Loud, *very* familiar music. She reached the edge of the alcove which was larger than it had appeared. A small paper calendar hung on a wall under a clock and several handwritten notices taped and pinned to the wall. The calendar was displaying June. She thought that was odd, since it was March, then she froze. On the cardboard top of the tear-away calendar, it said 1956. There was a roaring in her ears and she put her hand on the wall to steady herself. What? 1956? This wasn't possible.

The rushing-water sound in her ears subsided and she stepped around a stool to find a black curtain. The music. She knew this music. This was a very young Elvis singing "Hound Dog." Where was she? Her hands were shaking as she pulled the curtain slightly, peeking around the edge. There he was, in a gray oversized sport coat, dark pants, and dark shoes, performing "Hound Dog" on a stage. Dear God, she thought, she was backstage! Where was this? By the clothing he wore, she began to formulate a theory that she was witnessing his famous rendition of that song on the Milton Berle Show. This was the famous performance she often taught about in class because it had such staggering ramifications. It was this performance that sealed him as "obscene" and "vulgar." She staggered backward and leaned against the wall as the music ended. She could hear Elvis talking with another male voice, but it was muffled. The audience was laughing. Jenna felt as if the floor was turning to Jell-O and she might fall through it. She pressed her face against the cool wall, willing herself not to pass out or fall down. She had to get out of here. This wasn't real. It couldn't be.

She turned very deliberately and carefully and retraced her steps back to the janitor's closet. Maybe if she went back in there, she could escape this. What was happening? Was she *actually* in 1956? Dear God, what if she got stuck here? She closed the door behind her and sat down on the stool. Resting her face in her hands, she made an effort to breathe calmly and steadily, to get her rising freak-out under control. She heard more music, more crowd-of-people sounds. This couldn't be happening.

After what seemed like an eternity, she had herself under control and felt more normal. Her hands had stopped shaking and she was trying to reason through what her next move should be. If those men had dumped her in 1956, then she was going to have to figure out what to do. She fleetingly thought about the fact that her grandma was alive... Could she find her and make her understand? What on earth could she possibly say to make this sound even remotely plausible?

She heard a commotion of a group of people approaching the closet. She got up and opened the door, standing just inside the threshold, looking down the hall. Elvis and his entourage turned the corner, walked down the hall, and as he passed, he looked over. A faintly quizzical look crossed his face as their eyes met. She saw Scotty Moore and Bill Black just behind him and some faces she didn't know. Then the group was gone, around the corner, out of sight.

The tingling began again, and she clenched her fists and squeezed her eyes shut. She felt the shove from behind, and again the sensation of spinning. She crashed onto a hard surface on the same, already-sore shoulder, rolled and stopped.

"*Son* of a…" she said loudly, opening her eyes in her own kitchen. She looked up and saw her refrigerator behind her and Bill and Chris in the doorway, peering anxiously at her.

Jenna sat up, holding her now very painful shoulder, and leaned against the fridge. Bill came in cautiously, as though he feared her ability to reach him. "Sorry about the landing part," he said, concern on his face. "We can't control the physical position you're in. We have found, however, that leaving from a sitting position can often help a little with the fall."

Jenna glowered at him. "Super. Thanks for the heads up." She took his extended hand and hauled herself to her feet. She swayed a little and the nausea sloshed her stomach. Bill put his hands out to catch her.

"I'm fine," she said, leaning on the counter. She held the walls as she made her way to the couch and sat down. "Damn," she said. "That was… Was that real? I mean, what just happened?"

Bill and Chris sat in their respective chairs and leaned forward, elbows on their knees, obviously searching her face for evidence of her continued health.

"It was definitely real," said Bill, a small smile playing at his lips. "We sent you back to 1956. Did you see what we sent you to see?"

Jenna nodded slowly. "Well, briefly, yeah. You landed me in a janitor's closet, and I had no idea what I was supposed to be seeing. So, yeah."

Chris chuckled. "We know from hard-won experience about those landings. Sorry about not warning you. And we can only get with within about 10–15 feet of accuracy about where to set you down."

Bill looked sheepish. "Sorry about that. We wanted to set you down backstage. Didn't anticipate the closet."

Jenna blinked, then got up and walked over to the window bench and sat down. She glanced at the door to her tiny balcony at the end of the window seat, but as she was seriously questioning her ability to stay balanced, decided against stepping outside where there was potentially a two-story drop. The enormity of what had happened to her hit. Her eyes filled and she suddenly had difficulty getting air.

"Dear God," she whispered, almost to herself. "I *saw* him. I…looked into his… I *saw* him." She felt light-headed again. "I can't… I don't… I…," she trailed off, unable to form a coherent thought. This man, this singer. She had loved him since her earliest memory. Her mom, a huge fan, had inadvertently instilled this passion in her and he had become her go-to for everything. His music had formed the soundtrack of her life.

"I was a pretty lonely kid," she said, standing and walking to the balcony door. She stared out, seeing nothing, speaking to no one in particular. "I was an only child, and after about age seven or so, I had fairly disinterested parents. Elvis became my solace. Bad day? Elvis. Good day? Elvis. Happy? Elvis. Lonely? Elvis." She crossed her arms and looked at the two men. "To actually to have *seen* him…with… With my own eyes, even for a moment…" She stopped as her voice cracked and her throat felt lumpy. "You just don't know what that means to me, that's all," she finished, turning back to the door.

"We need to save him," said Bill softly, interrupting her thoughts. "He's been picked for a reason. Months and months of speculation, of playing out scenarios with dozens and dozens of people. Multiple jumps back into other eras, other times, to see literally dozens of potential candidates in person. This…this emotion—this passion—that he evokes in people… It's singularly special. It's absolutely powerful. It's like a force of nature—completely a phenomenon like no other. You're feeling it right now. There isn't anyone else *ever* who mesmerized people the way that man could. He is literally woven into our DNA." He rose and took a few steps toward Jenna. "Will you do this?"

The silence settled again, more gently this time. This silence wasn't dampening. It was quiet and soft, as if the universe knew she needed a few moments inside her head.

"How long was I gone?" she asked finally, not turning around.

"In 1956 time, about an hour. In 2022 time, about 3.5 minutes," said Chris.

"Why the discrepancy?"

"We're not actually sure why the time difference exists. It's consistent with every jump, though—that we are sure of."

Jenna turned and went back to the couch. "Explain your plan to me." She paused and put up her hand at them. "I mean *explain* it, like I'm in kindergarten."

They explained. Bill and Chris took turns as they walked her though what they wanted to do. The plan and design were carefully mapped out: they would retrieve Elvis from his Vegas gig in 1969 and send him here. After his arrival, he would spend three days holed up here with her, happy about it or not (they suspected not), while she made him understand what needed to change once he got back. Jenna would have no prohibitions—she could use any tool available to get her message through to him. No knowledge was off limits—he was to be told everything that exists as fact now. Nothing should be held back—pictures, videos, books; she could employ whatever she felt would be useful. Show him the results of his current choices. *Make* him see. *Make* him know. Elvis had a long history of refusing to face unpleasant realities. Jenna would have to fight her way through that, and his temper was legendary. She'd have to endure that, and so much else to get him to the other side. She would have to lay bare some brutal, *very* uncomfortable realities in very clear language. If she was successful, the ripples and altered destinies would affect his family, his career, and everything he touched, and by extension, society as a whole. The outcome could be absolutely staggering—changing the fates and trajectories of everyone he knew, family and friends alike.

She nodded slightly every so often, gazing at the coffee table. Could any of this be real? Her mind said absolutely not, but she had *seen* him. He walked right by her. What other explanation was there? And she certainly couldn't deny her physical experience when she jumped.

Jenna became aware of a lull in their explanations. She looked up and saw them sitting expectantly.

"I'm sorry, what?"

"I said, so what do you think?"

What *did* she think? Jenna had no idea. She knew they were right about the force this one man had to elicit emotion, devotion, and love. She knew there had never been anyone—ever—with the...the power he had. Forty-four years after his death, his fans and large swaths of the general public still held him up as the gold standard. His records sold. His movies still aired. A biopic about his life was currently being filmed. Hundreds of thousands flocked every year to see his home, his grave.

"What will he retain?"

"Everything, just as you did."

Quiet descended again. Jenna saw his eyes again in her mind. Blue. Tired. So much going on behind them. An old soul housed there.

"Okay," she murmured. "Okay."

Bill sighed audibly and Chris let out a small yelp. "Thanks, oh, thank you," they both stammered.

"What if I can't reach him? What if I'm never able to get through to him?"

"Then nothing particularly changes, does it? He goes back to '69 and convinces himself he dreamed it or something, and 1977 isn't altered. We have virtually nothing to lose by attempting this."

Jenna guessed not. Chris was heading out the door to fetch something from the car while Bill laid out the particulars. Elvis, as previously stated, would be snatched from his Vegas hotel and plopped unceremoniously into her apartment. They would have around three days to hash through the jungle of his future, which, to him, didn't exist yet. When he was ready to return, she would simply text the desired destination to a provided number, and they'd do the rest. She was free to jump with him to a past time, if she thought it would help. There was a landline to call instead of texting a location. She, because of this limitation, could not jump to any time that did not have telephones. Bill apologetically told her that the future wasn't possible yet either. He reminded her that if she went back, her cell phone, obviously, would not work.

"What if he stays past the three days?"

"Umm, well, that's not all the way tested, so we don't actually know," Bill said. "Keep it to the three-day timeline."

"Here is a caveat, though," said Bill. Jenna looked up. "If you're successful, we will be able to keep you on the current trajectory of time for *a while*. But not indefinitely. Eventually your understanding and consciousness will *have* to merge with the now-altered reality of him living past 1977."

"What does that mean, exactly?"

"It means that for a while, when this is all the way over, you will remember only the reality you live in now. Over the course of about a month, the changed reality will, for want of a better term, seep in and replace what you currently know. Given your birthdate, if this works, you'll never have known a time when he died young. That reality will have to eventually take over for you."

"What about him? Will he retain that there was, at one point, a different reality?"

"Yes. Because it's happening *to* him."

Jenna nodded and thought this over. "My memories of my life, my Nan, everything, will be gone?"

"No, they'll be replaced. Your whole life will have been lived with Elvis alive and well, and your replaced understanding will reflect that."

Chris came back through the door carrying a blue duffel bag and a guitar case.

"What's that?" Jenna asked.

"Stuff for him." Chris said. He unzipped the bag and pulled out pants, a few shirts, socks, etc. There was a container of his cigars, and some large pill bottles. At Jenna's raised eyebrows, he replied, "You want him in withdrawal here with you?" Jenna stated that she indeed did not.

"Remember that outside these walls he doesn't really exist. He's been dead for almost half a century in this time. He'll have no identity, no money, no understanding of the current world or technology. He's also very sheltered in his own time. There is a huge amount in 1969 he doesn't do for himself. So he's not as 'worldly' as you might think he is."

"Yes, I know. What if he just storms out? It's not like I can stop him."

"Obviously not, but follow him. You can drive him around, certainly, but he has no ability for an Uber, a cab, a flight, or even a bus. He has no identity, nothing."

Jenna nodded. "When will this…happen?"

"Tomorrow morning."

"What time?"

"No idea. It will depend on what he's doing at the time we choose to grab him up. So be ready. Also, if something goes wrong, the cell I gave you can also allow us to read a text question or request for help."

"Okay."

"You're all set."

"I guess…I think?"

"Text that number if you need anything or think of another question."

"I will."

The men opened the door and paused. "Thank you for agreeing to do this, Ms. Logan."

She looked into Bill's intense brown eyes and nodded wordlessly. They stepped out and the door clicked shut. Jenna was alone with a duffel full of Elvis Presley's stuff and a flopping stomach. Maybe this is where she would wake up?

3

With a lurch and an audible gasp, Jenna awoke. She looked around and realized she'd fallen asleep on the couch, TV on mute. The large-screen TV, one of the splurges she treated herself to a few years ago, was, oddly, showing a marathon of "Quantum Leap."

She stood up, and, heading for the bathroom, she stole a peek at the duffel bag and guitar case. They were still there, on her window bench where she'd set them last night. She had not touched them since, and there they sat. So she *hadn't* dreamed all of this. It actually happened.

On her way from the bathroom to the kitchen to make a pot of coffee, she pulled up her sleeve and made sure the two numbers she'd been given were there, in permanent marker, on her arm, underneath the Elvis tattoo on her forearm. Should she retrace them? They were also screenshotted into her photos and written on paper and stuck to her fridge.

Coffee brewing, she jumped into a fast shower and put on clean clothes. She nervously looked at the clock as she brushed out the long strawberry-blond hair down her back and saw that the clock read 8:20 a.m. She coiled her hair into a haphazard knot, secured it with a large clip, stepped into her fleece slippers, and headed back to the kitchen.

Coffee in hand, she shuffled into the small area with her tiny dining table and sat down to open her laptop. Sipping her hot coffee, she scanned news sites for any headline or information that might confirm she was insane, or that yesterday actually happened. Some sort of bizarre power surge? Sun flares causing hallucinations? Chemical leaks? She sighed when she saw nothing and meandered to her beloved window bench. She moved the duffel and guitar to the floor, then sat down and leaned against her Elvis pillow. She began taking a mental inventory of the food she had in the house. A recent trip for groceries made her confident she could feed him sufficiently. He'd want food, right? Her stomach flopped over.

It was then that she began to notice a faint buzz coming from her bedroom: kind of a vibrating hum. Her cell was on her lap and remained dark and silent. What was that? The hum grew louder and she felt like she was at a loud concert where the bass was hitting her in the chest. She jumped and squealed at the loud *thud* she heard from her room, then quiet.

A muffled "God *damn* it" came from the same place as the humming. She knew. He was here.

She shivered as she slowly but steadily walked to the bedroom door and peered in. On the floor between the bed and the wall was a shock of dark hair, and a hand on the back of the hair.

Jenna's hands were shaking and she felt cold and wobbly. The black hair rose as the man got to his feet, unaware that someone else was in the doorway. He lurched to his right and put his hand out on the bed to steady himself. She appraised his dark (brown?) pants and printed paisley shirt, his back still to her. Gaining his balance once again, she could see him starting to look around the room. She needed to make her presence known. She cleared her throat quietly.

He whirled around like a cornered tiger, putting his hands on the wall again for more balance. Jenna saw raw, jagged fear and utter confusion on the most abjectly beautiful face she'd ever looked at. The pictures she had seen all her life didn't even come *close* to capturing the essence of this man before her. He was, as Jenna's awed brain grappled for a word, magnificent. She involuntarily sucked in her breath and put her hand to her mouth.

"Wha…" he trailed off, looking dizzy again.

Jenna found her voice and stepped forward one step, hands out, hoping to demonstrate that he had nothing to fear.

"Hi. Umm… Hi? Okay, yeah. Hi. Umm… I'm Jenna." She stopped, hands still out, waiting.

He stared, his blue eyes flashing, his jaw set. He looked slightly dazed, but very wary. "Jenna who?"

He spoke. There was the voice. Dear God, that voice. Her stomach turned to jelly. "Umm. Jenna. Jenna Logan."

"Who are you? Where is this? What the *hell* is going on?" He took a few steps toward her, and she could see his stomach flop again. He sank onto the foot of her bed. Jenna took one more step closer, but still made sure she was a safe distance away.

"Well, umm (Stop saying umm!), you're in my apartment."

He rubbed a hand up and down his face. "Which is where, exactly?" He looked at her very squarely.

"Memphis—Germantown."

He nodded and looked past her, then his eyes snapped back to her face. A slow recognition registered in his eyes, and she saw that quizzical expression again. "Have we met? Do I know you?"

Jenna was very uncomfortable under his intense scrutiny. She laced her fingers together and twisted them until it hurt, then twisted them in the opposite direction.

"Well, sort of." She turned and walked back to the door. "I have some coffee on. Why don't you have some?" She walked into the kitchen, stomach fluttering, wondering what he'd do now. The green coffee cup clanked on the cabinet door as she nearly dropped it. She poured the cup full, marveling that she hadn't dropped the coffee pot, then turned to the fridge for the creamer. Realizing the sugar bowl was still out on the coffee table from yesterday—*Could that have been only yesterday?*—she went out to the table to get it. She turned back around and rattled the bowl and spoon, nearly dropping them when she saw Elvis at the door, partly into the small hallway. He didn't speak but seemed to have regained most of his balance. She mentally remarked again at the almost unfathomable presence of this impossibly handsome man. He generated his own electricity.

"I poured you a cup," she said stupidly, then walked past him back into the kitchen. She came within three feet of him, and he didn't flinch or step back. He followed her visually, but still said nothing. He seemed frozen. She was pulling a spoon out of the drawer when she felt a rough hand on her shoulder, jerking her around. She found herself facing a visibly angry and still somewhat scared Elvis, glowering and glaring, his eyes shooting daggers.

"What is this?" he demanded. "Who *are* you?" He must have seen fear flash across Jenna's face, as he removed his hand from her upper arm immediately and put it on his hip. He didn't budge, however, and stood looming over her, silently expecting a response.

Jenna shimmied sideways, disliking the sensation of being trapped between her kitchen sink and Elvis Presley's anger.

"Jenna Logan, as I told you." She pushed his cup of coffee toward him a little, motioned to the creamer and sugar, then stepped around him to return to the living room. She retrieved her own cup from the dining table, then sat on the couch, proud of herself that she hadn't burst into tears or passed out yet. She feared both options were still very much on the table. She could see his face over the breakfast bar counter, and his eyes shifted downward and the coffee cup was brought near his face as he smelled it. Apparently deciding it wasn't toxic, she heard the creamer top pop open, then the *clink clink clink* of stirring. A moment later he stepped through the kitchen door and cautiously perched on the chair across the coffee table from her. He sipped once, directly above the cup's handle, then set the cup down, staring at her. His eyes briefly scanned the living room, then back to Jenna. He got back up, walked around the table to her, and poked her shoulder, observed her closely, then poked it again. She watched him make sure that his hand wouldn't pass through her as if she were some sort of malevolent spirit. He returned to his seat and fingered his coffee cup absently.

"Okay," he said, leaning slightly forward. "What the hell has happened, and why do I know you? I've seen you…" His eyes registered recognition. "Wait. You were the one standing in the closet door after I was on Milton Berle. I walked past you!"

Jenna nodded, smiling. His face clouded and his brows knit slightly. "But how is that possible? That was what—13, 14 years ago? How can you look *exactly* the same?"

Jenna guessed she'd just jump right in and see if either of them could swim. "Because it wasn't 14 years ago. It was yesterday." She watched him closely. His eyes didn't flicker or move from hers for a moment.

"Yesterday."

"Yep."

"Okay. Sure." Elvis looked around and slapped his hands onto his knees. "Okay, honey, what's the prank? Who's playing this joke? Because it's not very funny."

Jenna stared, searching for what to say. "It's not a joke. There's no prank."

He nodded, looking increasingly irritated. Jenna asked him what year it was, and he looked at her incredulously. He told her it was 1969.

Jenna quietly said, "No. It's not. It's 2022 and you've come quite a long way."

"Sure. 2022. Okay." Elvis stood up and said, "Enough. Not funny. Time to stop. *Now*."

"Look," said Jenna, hoping the modern cars outside would start to convince him. He was obsessed with cars, so this might trigger some ability to hear the whole thing, or at least some kind of introduction. "Look outside. What do you see?" They stood at the balcony door.

He looked at her, then back outside. His face changed to uncertainty. "Those are cars…" he trailed off. She saw him trying to process how different they looked. A muscle in his jaw flexed and relaxed as he tried to make sense of this new information.

"Yes. Current cars. The blue Jeep down there? See? That's my car. It's a 2020 model." She pointed. "And think about the tingling and spinning and the crash landing in my bedroom. How did I 'prank' that? You actually experienced that, didn't you?"

After another moment of reflecting, he abruptly turned to her. Hands on his hips, he said, "Okay, honey. Tell me this whole story." Then he walked over and sat down, looking at her steadily. Jenna knew he was no more ready to hear this than she was yesterday morning, but she joined him and sat on the couch.

"What do you want to know?"

"First off, who are you?"

"Jenna Logan. I'm 37. I was born in February of 1985. I'm an associate professor at U of M. I teach a course about the greatest societal influences of the 20th century. I teach a large portion of a whole semester about you."

"Married?"

"Not anymore."

"Kids?"

"Nope."

"You from here?"

"Nope. St. Louis."

"So is that what this is? You've…got me here because you want to…" He trailed off but never once looked away.

"Want to?" Jenna didn't have any idea what he meant. Then it clicked.

"Oh, gawd," she said, standing back up. "Get *over* yourself." She went and stood by the window bench.

"You're the one who brought me here. Is this some sort of kidnapping thing?"

"I did *not* 'bring you here.'" Jenna used air quotes. "I had nothing to do with how you arrived, or even *that* you arrived."

"Then what *is* this?" he demanded. His temper flared and he marched toward her. "How did I get here, and what do you want from me?"

Jenna refused to flinch, even though her mind urged her to back away from a visibly angry man whose temper was legendary. She made herself stand still, facing him.

"I'm Jenna Logan. I told you this."

"What do you want?" He was less than 18 inches from her, clearly angry. Traces of fear were still scattered through his eyes, however, which Jenna grabbed onto to keep herself from calling this whole thing off. She breathed slowly and deeply, looking intently at his shirt buttons, willing herself to remain in control.

"What I want is for you to not die. That's it. That's all I want. That's the goal here. I want you to absorb the enormous amount of information I have been asked to give you, then I want you to *not die!*" She was breathing faster than she wished and hoped he didn't notice. When he didn't immediately respond, she looked up into his face. The anger had receded some, and a faint smile pulled at his mouth.

"Honey, do I look like I'm dying?"

Jenna sighed in exasperation, and she felt a slight irritation creeping in about being called "honey" repeatedly. She realized he was from a different era, a different place, but that term felt condescending and was starting to get on her nerves. Elvis was not going to make this easy. She stalked around him and moved toward the dining table, then turned to face him.

"No, you do not. And stop calling me 'honey,'" she said through clenched teeth. "I have stuff… Information you need to know." She bristled internally as he gave her a patronizing little smile.

"Oh *do* you…"

"Yes," she hissed. "I do."

"Such as?"

"Such as you're fine now, mostly, but the pills you're currently taking are going to hurt you. A *lot*." She watched his self- assured smile falter imperceptibly. "You live to be 42 years old. You died on August 16, 1977, in your bathroom. At Graceland. Lisa was in the house. She saw the chaos."

His face clouded and then turned to anger. "*Enough* of this shit!" he spat. He turned and walked into her bedroom and slammed the door.

Jenna deflated and sank into the computer chair. She rubbed her face and sat, staring at the dark screen. She was going to have to show him pictures. Pictures of himself, so sick he could hardly stand up. Videos of himself, trying to get enough air to sing, to perform. He needed proof. A long, tired sigh escaped from her soul. God, she was weary. Losing Nan wasn't enough? Now this? Lovely, sweet Nan—the whole, original source of the Elvis obsession. How she missed her. It ached and her eyes stung as she remembered her gentle smile and unwavering devotion to her only grandchild. Where would she be without her Nan? What, Jenna wondered, would she tell her to do now? She *had* to get this bullheaded man to understand his fate. Today was day one. She only had three to make another human change his habits, outlook, desires, and entire life course. Impossible. She was suddenly sure this couldn't be done.

She knew, on some level, what he was doing in her bedroom because she had done the same thing in 1956 when she scuttled back to the janitor's closet. He was sitting on the floor where he'd landed, praying to be sent back or to wake up from this madness that was scaring him. Jenna didn't blame him. This was terrifying, as she well knew, having just experienced it herself. And in all honesty, who was she to him? A total stranger who seemed to be completely insane, that's who. She felt like a parent trying to wait out a sullen teenager who'd taken to his bedroom to sulk. Well, she thought, Elvis was pretty well known to like women in his life to "mother" him. His reclamation, his redirection of his soul and his life, literally and figuratively, was her task. He didn't want this, he didn't ask for this, and he didn't believe he needed it. She could hear Nan telling her that things were going to get worse before they got better. Great. Why had she agreed to do this? All of this before 10:00 a.m. was too much. Long day ahead, she decided. Again—just great.

Well, if he wasn't coming out in the immediate future, she could at least eat something herself. She plodded to the kitchen and began fishing around in the fridge. Eggs, sausage, and cheese came out and she set everything on the counter. New pot of coffee started, she began cracking eggs, enough for two people just in case, pausing every so often to listen for any movement from the bedroom. Silence. Sausage patties were starting to sizzle, and she popped a small can of biscuits open and put the pan in the oven. She returned to the eggs, zoning out as the fork *tink tink tinked* on the stainless steel bowl as she scrambled them. She wondered vaguely if he was still a little queasy, and if all this food might make it worse. *That'd be perfect*, she thought.

Good job, Jenna. Take an awful, impossible situation and make it worse. She rolled her eyes at herself. She rummaged through her kitchen junk drawer and pulled out some wrapped utensils for him. She was sure she remembered he didn't like to use silverware at other people's houses and usually brought his own.

As she flipped the sausage a final time, she heard the bedroom door open. She paused, then plopped some butter in the pan for the eggs, and turned on the heat. She tensed as she became aware that he was standing in the doorway, looking at her.

"More coffee?" she asked, desperately hoping that forcing herself to not look up would make her appear nonchalant instead of twisted into knots. And why, exactly, did he have to be this incredibly good looking? She reminded herself that he was her Nan's age.

He slid around to the breakfast bar opposite her and perched on the high chair. She knew he was watching her intently. Instead of waiting for an answer, she poured a fresh cup and slid it across the counter to him. She began scrambling the eggs and took the sausage off the heat.

"Who are you really?" he asked, accusation in his voice.

"I told you who I am. Jenna Logan." She walked out to the laptop table, got her wallet out of her purse, then walked back to the kitchen. She opened her wallet and pulled out her driver's license, then slid it over to him. "Jenna. Logan," she said again.

He was silent again, but he sipped the coffee as he looked at her license. At least it didn't appear that he feared she was poisoning him. She put the ID back in her wallet and took two plates, one fork, and the wrapped utensils out and set them on the bar counter with the plate of sausage. She mixed the cheese into the eggs to melt. The biscuits were done, so she turned off the oven and placed a spatula and the butter dish by the pan. Eggs dumped into a bowl, she put them up onto the bar as well, then began to serve herself, neither of them speaking.

"Aren't you hungry?" she asked, finally looking at him square in the face. His jaw was set—she could see a muscle flexing in his cheek. He was staring at her, his face almost but not quite angry. His eyes darted to the plate and his posture loosened slightly. He turned and picked up the other plate and began to help himself. His back to her, she sighed and felt weak as she moved herself to the living room to eat. She realized her hands were trembling. She bit into a sausage as he set his plate and cup down on the coffee table across from her. He sat, motionless, looking at her.

Finally she was so self-conscious that she stopped chewing. "What?" she asked, knowing what a ridiculous thing that was to ask.

He took a bite of eggs, still silent and watching her. His eyes flicked to his plate, then back at her.

"These are good. I like the cheese." He took another bite as if to prove his sincerity.

"Glad you like them," Jenna said quietly. "So…" She looked at him. "I would imagine you have… More questions?" Silently he nodded, picking up a sausage.

"Well, I can answer as much as I know."

He nodded again.

Jenna proceeded to relay the last three days to him, starting with Nan's death, and her realization that she was being followed, and that they had been watching her for quite a long time. As they ate, she described the visit from Chris and Bill, what they told her, and the whole experience of being sent back, where he saw her in the closet doorway. She talked, rather animatedly, for 20 minutes as they finished breakfast. He didn't utter a sound—he just sat wordlessly, chewing, watching her. She finally finished with "…and there you were, on my bedroom floor." She leaned back and was quiet.

Elvis pushed back his plate and drained the rest of his coffee, then he too sat back, returning her gaze. He said nothing.

"That is literally the whole story up to now," she said, hoping to spur some sort of dialogue. After a moment, she said, "You don't believe me."

A small smile tugged his lips upwards and he shook his head. "Not really."

"Okay, I get that. But explain what *physically* happened to you that dumped you onto my floor. What were you doing when the tingling started?"

"I was standing backstage, going over some changes I was thinking about for tonight's show."

"Were you alone?"

"Yeah, at that moment I was."

"And *poof*!" Jenna made little exploding hand motions. "You just magically landed here."

"No, there was all that spinning and someone shoved me. And that freaky tingle feeling."

"Why do you not believe your own body? You *know* you got transported here in a way you can't explain." She stood up and began clearing the dishes. She set them in the sink and glanced at him through the breakfast bar. He had a fingernail on his teeth, staring at his feet, obviously deep in thought.

She walked out and picked up her laptop, and went back to the couch. His eyes grew large as he looked at it. He stared at the device as though it were a mixture of a striking cobra and a wonder from heaven.

"This is a computer. A laptop. Everyone has one nowadays. It's connected to the internet." Jenna tried her best to explain this concept, and pulled up pictures of his Vegas show that he was literally in the middle of. She turned the screen around to face him and watched his eyes grow even larger.

"Look familiar?" she asked. Still wordless, he nodded imperceptibly.

"I…that…" he stammered. "That was two nights ago."

"Not really, actually," she said, turning the laptop back to face her. "It was really 53 years ago. Today is March 9th, 2022. You left in early August of 1969, correct?" Again he nodded slightly, staring at the back of the laptop. His mind was visibly racing as he struggled to make sense of this.

Jenna pulled up still photos of the following year in Vegas when *That's The Way It Is* was filmed.

"This is 1970. They filmed a movie called *That's The Way It Is.*" It looked as if his eyes would literally bulge from their sockets. He leapt up and glided around the coffee table, sat down next to her, and snatched the laptop. He held it up, looked under and around it, then set it back down and ran his fingers lightly over the keyboard and then the screen.

Jenna paused, unsure if she should do what was occurring to her. She decided to go ahead and pulled up a current picture of Lisa Marie. She said nothing, just let him look. He was still examining the charging cord when his eyes snapped to the screen, recognition flashing across his face. She saw immediately that he knew he knew this woman but couldn't say why.

"Who is that?"

"Your daughter. That's Lisa as she looks now, in 2022." Elvis stared at the screen, seemingly mesmerized.

"She looks like her mother..." he whispered. "God, she's beautiful. My God." He lightly touched the screen.

"She is indeed beautiful. But many say she looks like her father." Elvis continued to stare for another moment, then looked at Jenna.

"Is this real? I...I don't... Is it?" He poked her arm again, trying to make sense of this.

Jenna nodded. "It is. You're here. I'm here. It's 2022. You've... You've been dead 44 years, Elvis."

He drew in a ragged breath and his eyes filled. He stood up and walked over to the window bench. "You say I...that I died..." He choked out a "How?" before wiping his face.

Jenna's heart ached for him. Who could possibly hear all this without feeling absolute devastation? The worst was yet to come.

"Heart attack," she said softly.

He nodded, continuing to stare out the window, clearly attempting to get himself under control. "That's...young..." he trailed off.

"Yeah. It was. You were... You were *really* sick, Elvis, and had been for a long time. The drugs had taken over and..."

Elvis didn't turn around, but his voice was more in command now, and it had a slightly flinty edge. "I'm not some sort of junkie."

"No, you're not. But you're an addict. And if you're not now, you will be shortly." He turned, eyes flashing. He walked back to her.

"Prove it," he challenged. "I know exactly what I take, why, why it helps, and all the effects."

"Do you? You sure about that?" Jenna asked as she pulled up a picture of his final concert in June of 1977. "You *absolutely* sure, Elvis?"

He froze and recoiled from the photo. "Wha... What..." he garbled, staring in disbelief. Jenna rode this wave and clicked the video of his rendition of "Unchained Melody"—the last performance of his life. He watched, his eyes wide, a look of abject horror on his face. He could not deny this. It was clearly him. It was clear that he was desperately ill.

And he knew absolutely that nothing like this had happened to him to date. He put a hand over his mouth and watched, as though he wanted to run but couldn't.

"That beautiful voice," Jenna whispered.

"No...I... No," he said, not looking away from himself on the screen. The video ended and he sat in stunned silence, his hand still over his mouth. "This is some sort of trick photography... Some kind of... That's not me..."

"It is. It *is* you. You died two months later," she told him. "The world was stunned. The grief was worldwide." She clicked a photo of his funeral procession in Memphis, then on pictures of the news headlines from all over. "Tens of thousands came, Elvis."

He was again shocked into silence. He looked like he'd just been kicked in the stomach, and Jenna worried for a moment he might throw up. He sucked in his breath and looked closely at the picture of his daughter in knee socks at his funeral.

She reached out on impulse and lightly touched his hand. "I'm so sorry about this. I can't imagine how terrible this must be for you."

He removed his hand from her, definitively but without anger, and stood up again. He walked, looking somehow older, over to the balcony door, opened it, and stepped out. Jenna's heart lurched. He surely wouldn't jump...and...was it possible for him to die? He was already dead. Wasn't he? Or no?

She followed him outside. The cold air felt kind of refreshing. She sat next to him on the other chair, saying nothing.

"Where's Priscilla?" he asked, not looking at her. He seemed to be fixated on a spot in the distance. Jenna told him about how she was the driving force behind saving Graceland, how his estate was nearly bankrupt, and how her overriding work now was ensuring his lasting legacy. She told him of her subsequent career in acting, her second child, and that to this day, his legacy is of utmost importance to her. He absorbed her words quietly.

"And my father?"

Jenna told him, and about his grandmother, whom he lovingly called "Dodger." He closed his eyes, a single tear falling, and he resumed his observation of a far-off point. They sat in silence for what seemed like hours, feeling a chilly breeze, ignoring the cold, just processing a vast, unfathomable cache of information.

Elvis broke the silence at last, turning to her. "So, we split up? 'Cilla left me?"

Jenna nodded. "In '72. Your divorce was final in October of '73."

"For another man?"

"Oh, only sort of. Not really. I mean, yeah, there was someone else, but he wasn't the primary reason why she left. He was more of a result than a cause." Jenna paused, weighing her next comment. "I mean, how much was she supposed to take?"

He continued to look at her, very steadily. "Take?"

"Well, yeah. The other women, and the increasing drug use and..." Jenna looked directly into his eyes. "She's a human being, Elvis. Not your servant, sent to do your bidding. She had, and *has,* dreams, hopes, wants, passions. She wants to grow and develop as a person. She deserved better than sitting at home while you...entertained others. She needed to experience the world on *her* terms, with *her* needs in mind."

Elvis winced slightly and sought out his distant focal point. She expected him to lash out at this, but he was quiet. It seemed to Jenna that his shoulders sagged a little.

"I love her, you know. I just...I...don't know."

"She loves you too. She gave you her life. Every minute of it."

The quiet settled back, and Jenna stood up to go back in. The chill was causing her to shiver. Still staring ahead, he said to no one in particular, "I would never do anything to hurt her or Lisa."

"Well. That's why you're here, isn't it? To fix that?" Jenna asked, then she went inside and closed the door, leaving him with his thoughts.

4

The rest of the day leaned into the need for information; the intense desire to understand purposes, outcomes, and intent. Upon reentering the apartment, his eyes fell upon Jenna's shelves and shelves of books. He had stepped hesitantly closer, and was perusing titles when she pointed out the books she owned about him. She had several, and his eyes grew wide as she stacked them in front of him. He picked up Priscilla's book, *Elvis and Me*, and examined the back cover.

"So many. Priscilla wrote a book about me... About us?"

"Yeah. I think everyone who ever even met you has written a book about you."

"I don't...I don't know what to think about that," he said, picking up a heavy volume. "*Last Train to Memphis*," he murmured, flipping through the pages.

"That's about your early life and rise to fame." Jenna said. "Here. This is the one that has the information you're wanting to know," she told him as she handed him the follow-up book, *Careless Love*. "This and the one Priscilla wrote should give you a lot of information."

Elvis took the books and drifted over to the window bench and began to read. Jenna loaded and started the dishwasher, completed some things online for her Nan's estate and for her leave of absence, then she went to the hall closet and began laundry in the stacking washer/dryer unit housed there. She saw Elvis intently staring at the unit as she loaded the clothes, but he returned to the reading.

The day passed in amiable silence, with Elvis registering quiet, periodic emotion to his discovery of more information. Jenna saw his eyes fill more than once, and he turned to look out the window. She couldn't even comprehend how disorienting and frightening this must be—to be ripped from a normal life, dropped into a stranger's space, and told it's more than 50 years into the future. Then to be told by that complete stranger that you're an addict destined for an early death.

His attention was diverted for a few minutes when she turned on the large TV, but she put it on mute and picked up a book of her own. Dark had fallen when she felt a cover being gently placed on her, and she drifted back into her nap for another moment. She gradually became aware that she was being watched. As she opened her eyes, she saw him, perched on the arm at the other end of the couch, watching her. She stretched and smiled.

"Sorry I dozed off."

"That's fine." He continued to look at her. "Why did you agree to do this?" His stare was intense, but without anger.

Jenna sat up. "Because you're important."

He shook his head and uttered a derisive snort. "No, apparently I'm not. It seems that I'm a jerk. A stone-cold asshole."

"Oh. How far did you get?"

"Around 1975. I was skimming some."

"Oh, okay. Only two more years." She looked down, instantly regretting having said that. Elvis got up and walked back to the balcony door. He looked like he might burst with pent-up emotion.

"It's like I'm poison, I guess? According to that, I ruined my career, my marriage, my relationships…"

"Well, *ruined* is a strong word, but overall, yes." Jenna couldn't say or do anything else. He spoke the truth.

"So, I'm an addict? I'm…some sort of druggie." He spat the last word.

"Not really, no. Not like you're thinking. You're someone who used medication to continue to function. To keep…being you. To literally stay upright. You have a lot wrong with you physically."

"I feel fine. I don't have anything wrong with me," he insisted.

"Really? Insomnia? Intestinal problems?"

He blushed and turned back to the window.

"In case you haven't gleaned it yet from the book, your biggest enemy wasn't your ailments, though they were pretty significant. It was your ego. Thinking—*insisting*—that you know every damn thing. You don't," she said as she got up and walked toward him.

Clearly annoyed by this statement, he didn't look at her when she reached him, but she could see the irritation in his jaw and posture.

"I know you don't want to hear that. I get it. No one wants to be told that. But it's true. That book you value so much, that desk reference? The one that makes you think you're some sort of doctor? It can't replace an actual doctor, who went to medical school. You aren't an expert. You *aren't* a doctor." She saw him wince a little, and his jaw became even more set. He said nothing. She waited a few moments, then went to the window bench. She pulled out her cell phone. "Want some dinner?"

He looked at her, his eyes resting on the phone. He walked over and stared at it.

"Cell phone," she said. "Think car phone? Brief case phone? But *much* more advanced." She used face ID, opened the phone, and handed it to him. He held it carefully, clearly not knowing what to do with this device.

"Here, look," she said, patting the seat beside her. He sat down next to her and she began swiping, scrolling, clicking, and demonstrating. She explained email, Apple Music, the internet. He stared, slack-jawed, as she explained modern phones, social media, and text messages.

After about 30 minutes of tutorial, she said, "Here, I'll also make a call." She dialed an Italian restaurant and ordered dinner to be delivered. "It's also just a regular old phone, too."

Dinner came and they split an order of lasagna and garlic bread, and they each drank a cold Pepsi. They talked, but it was mostly her answering his peppering of questions. Conversation turned to nostalgia—he asked about the Memphian Theatre, Lansky Brothers, and the Fairgrounds Amusement Park. He spoke of his mother, she spoke of her Nan.

His eyes grew misty and soft as he talked about his beloved mother, and Jenna could see this woman had meant everything to him. She was his safety, his sanity, his sounding board.

"It's been 11 years since she died. I still miss her so much. I still have days where I feel lost, and I want to see her face. Talk to her. Ask her what she thinks." He stopped and finished off his soda, then looked at Jenna.

"Why did your grandma play such a huge role? Where were your parents?" he asked her.

"They were just so…involved with being professors and academics that they seemed to forget they had a daughter. They traveled constantly, and I became kind of an afterthought. I think they loved me… They just didn't have time to be in their profession and my parents as well. The profession won. They're currently somewhere in Europe, I think. I stopped keeping track years ago."

Elvis nodded, swallowing a large bite of garlic bread.

"It's funny. You had nothing in material items but you had the unwavering, absolute devotion of your parents. I wanted for nothing materially, but would have given my left arm for the caring and concern from my parents like you had." Jenna said, picking at the last of her lasagna with her fork. Elvis nodded.

"And you were married?"

"Yeah for a while," she said. "We divorced about three years ago."

"Sorry," he said.

"Ah. Don't be. It wasn't ever going to last. I knew it even then, I think. I thought I could change him."

Elvis nodded, twisting his empty Pepsi bottle thoughtfully. He studied her, and Jenna could see he wanted to say something and was weighing whether he should. She finished her lasagna and sat back, looking at him.

"What we talked about earlier. I want to say again—I'm not a junkie. I actually *do* know what I'm doing."

"Uh-huh. Sure." Jenna nodded. She pulled out her phone and googled several photos of him from the '77 final concert. "That's nice. But does *he* know what he's doing? Because *he* seems to be struggling. A *lot*." She turned the screen to him, and his eyes narrowed. He took the phone, clearly horrified anew. He looked at who was clearly him, but must have seemed like a total stranger. His face registered distaste and fear. When he'd seen enough, he handed back the phone and sat in silence, brooding.

"Elvis, the drugs are the crux of the problem. The whole point of you being sent here is so you can see what happened and change course. Alter the choices that got you there."

His eyes filled again and he looked away, blinking. "I don't know how. I can't sleep. I've never been able to sleep."

"I know. So you rely on the pills to let you sleep. But then you need more to wake up. Then things hurt or ache, so there are more for that. Then more again to sleep, and the cycle perpetuates. They are, as you saw, taking over. You *cannot* control this,

Elvis. You *have* to stop, or all this will have been for nothing. Look what they did to you! Look what *you* did to you, all the while telling everyone you knew what you were doing!"

Jenna couldn't tell if he was actually hearing and processing her words. He stared at the floor, a blank expression on his face.

"There is kind of a new thought on this." His eyes lifted to hers. "That in '67 when you fell and hit your head so badly, you might have actually triggered an autoimmune response that plagued you for the rest of your life. I don't really know how valid that theory is medically. But modern medicine knows far more about autoimmune disease than '70s medicine, when they knew pretty much nothing. There are even murmurs that maybe your mom suffered from autoimmune hepatitis? That maybe it's genetic? I don't know. But the colon problems—I know that's embarrassing—but many painkillers are well documented now to cause extreme constipation. Add them to your already poor colon, and you have a disaster on your hands. Again, common denominator: the pills."

Jenna waited cautiously, afraid he'd storm out or start yelling. Instead he looked defeated and sad.

"Can we talk about this later? I don't even know what 'autoimmune' is, and I need to think about this."

Jenna nodded. "Wanna see what music and movies have been like?" She smiled, changing the subject to something she knew he'd like. He nodded and they went to settle on the couch. She turned the

TV back on and searched YouTube for videos. She showed him everything from Hootie and the Blowfish to Eminem. His eyes were huge and a little proud as she played for him the JXL version of "A Little Less Conversation" from 2002 and explained how well it had done on the charts. They spent until the wee hours watching video after video. She watched him solemnly absorb Desert Storm. She saw his heartache over 9/11. He was horrified by the footage of the Covid pandemic. She watched him absorb clips from Jaws, Star Wars, Jurassic Park, and Harry Potter. She laughed at his face when he watched Culture Club and Cyndi Lauper in the 80s. She watched his solemn respect when he heard Eddie Van Halen. The world since 1969 drifted by him in sound bites and video clips. He drank every moment in thirstily, waiting for more. Finally, after hours of traveling through history, she turned on 2005's *"Elvis By The Presleys"* for him, and he settled in to watch the people closest to him talk about him, and his life, and his death.

Jenna drifted off during the movie, satisfied that he was completely mesmerized. She wondered how utterly surreal it must be to watch your own life discussed and retold. At some point—Jenna didn't know when—she felt the weight shift on the couch and she felt fingertips against her fingertips. They both slept as the credits rolled and the screen went dark.

5

As Jenna paused in her storytelling, and they all adjusted their minds back to the present, Lisa stretched and stood up, loosening her hips while excusing herself for a bathroom break. Had Jenna really been telling this story for an hour and a half? Elvis also went to use the restroom and move around a little, leaving Jenna alone in the den. She looked at the gold records, the various framed awards—she was momentarily startled when several of them had dates after 1977. So much had changed. Her eyes fell onto the statue of the gold man. He'd won an Oscar for *A Star Is Born*, with Barbra Streisand. He had been able to take that role after all. She stared at that trophy, knowing how important it must be to him.

Elvis returned to the den, took Jenna's arm in his, and they stood quietly for a few minutes. He smiled at her as she stared at the award. "I was so scared of that movie I almost didn't do it. I have never been that terrified in my life as that first day of shooting. There was talk that I couldn't pull it off, that I was unable to muster that level of acting, and on and on. It was pretty easy to start believing."

"I can imagine. But no Colonel to stop it from happening. And you went for it!"

"I did. Grabbed it and tore into it. And you know, I'd forgotten about that first night after you hit me with some painful truths, then I saw a whole movie with everyone talking about me and some doses of my own stupidity. I just wanted human contact."

Jenna nodded. "I know. I'm glad you did. But you know, that whole movie was about more than your mistakes. It also showcased your immense accomplishments, and their love for you."

Elvis motioned to a smaller award and grinned. "Got this one too, following your advice. I did that movie in 2012 because I damn well wanted to. Playing the bad guy was a lot of fun."

Jenna squinted and read the little plaque with the Golden Globe. "You were Snow in Hunger Games?? Oh my gawd! I love those books! I completely missed that when I got back!"

She was genuinely thrilled. Elvis smiled and nodded, clearly pleased.

They moved back to their seats as Lorraine set out some more cold Pepsis and water and a plate of fruit and small cookies. Jenna nibbled a chocolate chip cookie. A scene flashed into her mind's eye. She was standing in an unfamiliar room, laughing and joking with Elvis, eating small appetizers from a tiny plate. He was holding the Golden Globe award and was joking about how fun it was to be the bad guy.

Jenna sat forward with a start. This had not happened—she didn't even know about this event. Where did this image come from? Had her mind created it in the last 60 seconds based on seeing the award? How could that be? The image was very vivid, complete with details of him, of the room, the sounds, the smells. She could even recall the taste of the small sausage appetizer she was eating. Her memory searched for the words Chris and Bill had imparted about the universe's timeline... What had he said? When she looked up, she saw Elvis watching her intently, his elbow resting on his cane, but he said nothing.

Elvis looked at the gold lion on the handle of his cane. "That was one of the hardest things I've ever done," he said quietly.

"The movies, or giving up the pills?" Jenna asked, still a little distracted by the image that was now fading from her mind. She felt about a half a bubble off center.

"Yeah." They both laughed. "Well, I didn't give them all up. They're monitored, and I'm on some to this day. But yeah, getting control of my life, of myself. Getting my health under my own control. God, it was a bad time. I spent weeks in the hospital so the press wouldn't find out about a drug rehab stay. Though I must admit, looking back on it, I'm pretty sure they knew exactly what was going on."

Jenna took his hand. "I'm so glad you did it."

"Me too."

"I had hoped it would change the dynamic with Priscilla."

"Oh it did," he said. "It absolutely did. We went on a getaway and we hashed through a lot. She laid some stuff out that I *really* didn't want to hear. There were fights and yelling and crying and talks, and we were both laid open to the bone. We tried it again, but in the end, with the stuff that happened, we couldn't quite make it. We were and are very close.

The love never wavered, and still hasn't. I love her *so* much. And she loves me. We just... Don't work as well married."

Jenna nodded. "I didn't see that you ever remarried."

Elvis shook his head. "I didn't. Neither of us did, actually. I came close twice, but in the end, it didn't happen."

"And your health was a tough road?"

"God, yes," he said, rolling his eyes. "I spent quite a while after I got back soul-searching. I reflected on all we'd talked about and about the path I was clearly on but didn't see until my little trip to see you. Or maybe I saw it and didn't want to. I don't know. But I decided to stop it before it got ugly, before I began to be that man in the pictures and videos you showed me. Those pictures haunted me, man. I could *not* get them out of my mind. I needed some control back. It had been *so* long since I felt like I had any kind of say-so or control after doing all the pictures. So, I went to Dr. Nick and laid out what I wanted. We came up with a plan and I followed it to the letter—and I still do. My diet changed. Well, mostly. I began seeing a psychiatrist, and later on, I even went on antidepressants for a little while. I started addressing issues I'd been running from since I lost my mom—anger, guilt, loss. And one of the worst parts was admitting I needed to do any of this. Just getting to that point damn near killed me-admitting all that. So we assembled a team for my eyes and for the intestinal problems. It was a long hard few years. But it was pretty successful. And here I am." He smiled that familiar smile and Jenna could only react by hugging him.

"And the Colonel?"

"Eh. That was another whole story." He chuckled. "I had always been content to let him handle everything, as you and I discussed. During all my soul-searching, I also had to decide if I was able—or even willing—to change not only my life expectancy, but also my career and professional life. I didn't make any drastic professional changes until after Aloha. I was feeling pretty good by then and had control of my own path. I had started to push back on things I didn't like, and there were a few really good fights. Confrontation is *not* my thing."

They both laughed. "The weird thing is, I never really 'confronted' the Colonel. I simply said, 'No, that's not good for me,' or 'This is what I plan to do and I'm moving forward with or without you.'"

Elvis paused and gazed into space for a moment. "He was upset that I retained an attorney to represent my interests. He was upset that I hired an accountant to manage my money, with oversight from my father. I was never sure why those things upset him, except that he felt I no longer trusted him, and he didn't have sole influence. Finally it came to a head in '73. After Aloha was released here, I flat-out said, 'I'm touring Europe.' He started listing the 5,000 reasons why we shouldn't, so I told him to stay back and I'd go. He refused. No, no, no, I wasn't going anywhere without him, what with security such a problem. What he *really* meant was he didn't want me drifting out of his control. He didn't know that by then there had been some digging around, and I'd already found out about his citizenship issues. So, we parted company. I wasn't even all that angry. I just...told him the decision had been made. I paid him some money to buy off what he claimed I owed him from the early days—not nearly what he wanted—and that was that. We didn't really communicate again. He signed releases relinquishing all future claims on me or my name, and we were done. I called his wife and sent flowers in '97 when he died."

Jenna nodded again, still clutching his hand. She couldn't even begin to articulate the joy and relief she felt right now. She was almost weak.

"How did all of you weather the pandemic?" Jenna asked.

"Oh, we did okay," Elvis said. "I had seen certain videos prior to the start of it..." He gave her a sly grin. "... and I had stocked up on a lot. Graceland had *plenty* of toilet paper."

Jenna laughed heartily at the vision of the confused looks he must have gotten when he ordered so much at once.

Suddenly she was aware of a backstage she knew she'd never seen before. In a flashing consciousness, she "saw" Elvis onstage, but from behind the large set up for the drums. He was wearing a two piece green and white suit, had white hair, and was laughing onstage about something. He was clearly about 70 years old. This had never happened. What was this? As suddenly as it had come, the flash of memory was gone, leaving Jenna feeling off kilter and internally starting to doubt her sanity. She had never been backstage at an Elvis concert. He had died 8 years before she was born. This green and white suit was unknown to her—she had never seen a photo of anything like that. What was this scene in her memory?

Lisa returned and sat back into her seat. She kicked her shoes off and tucked a foot under her to get comfortable.

"Okay. Where were we?"

6

Weak sunlight peeked in as Jenna awoke. Elvis was gone from the couch and it took her a second before she panicked. Where had he gone? He didn't exist! Oh no! She bolted off the couch and was charging into her bedroom when she realized the shower was running. Oh thank *God*. He was in the shower. She went into the kitchen to make some breakfast and found he'd figured out how to make coffee already. She smiled—that was unexpected. The water shut off with a squeak and she heard him humming and singing to himself through the door. Was humming a good sign for his mood? The door opened and he emerged, towel draped over his head, wearing the clothes Bill and Chris had left in the duffel. Jenna had completely forgotten about them.

He stopped in the kitchen doorway and motioned to himself. "These are my actual clothes. I found them in that blue bag over there. Who got these?" He motioned to the black pants and green button up shirt.

"Chris and Bill brought the bag, so I assume they did." She said. "You saw...everything in the bag?"

"Yeah. I did," he said. "Why did they bring all these pills if the goal is to get me to stop taking them?"

"Because sending you into withdrawal isn't conducive to you making intelligent life choices." Jenna laughed. Elvis smiled but looked troubled.

"What?" she asked.

"I wonder if anyone saw them. These were at the house. I wonder if they got in and out."

"Well, I would guess they pretty much did. No subsequent books discussed strange men in blazers running loose at Graceland. You know your grandma always said Graceland was haunted. Maybe they're who she heard as they jumped in to get your things." They both mused over this for a moment, then Jenna finished breakfast prep. They ate in amiable quiet, then Elvis said "Let's go out today. I want to see the house."

Jenna looked up from her cereal bowl. "You know you're dead, right?"

"Well, yeah, so wouldn't that make going out easy? I don't exist in this time, right?"

"Yeah…"

"So—who'd be looking for me? I'm dead!" Elvis grinned and tipped his chair back. "I could go anywhere I want! I can *do* anything I want!" He looked positively pleased with himself. "Do you know how long it's been since I could just…*go* somewhere? Freely? Just…get in the car and go where I want?"

"If you want to see Graceland," Jenna said, going to the coffee table for the laptop, "Look here first." She opened the laptop, plugged it in to charge, and opened two tabs, one for Graceland and one for Graceland Tours. He came and sat down and she showed him how to scroll and click between the two tabs, hit play, pause, etc. He watched closely as she opened a new tab and she showed him how to use a finger on the mousepad. She went to clean up and change her clothes while he perused the info on his house.

As she was getting out her clean clothes he called, "I have a *plane*? I bought an airplane??"

"Yes! You did!" Jenna called back as she pulled on her pants. "In 1975 you got the *Lisa Marie*, but you had, like, five, I think, altogether. I can't remember for sure."

"Lord have mercy." She heard him say to himself as he went back to the pages she'd opened for him.

Twenty minutes later she emerged with combed hair braided down her back, brushed teeth, and clean face and clothes. As she walked to the coffee table to clear the remaining dishes, she noticed Elvis was very quietly watching the screen, obviously upset. His eyes were welled and he was struggling to keep his composure. She walked up behind his chair and saw a paused video on the screen of a 1974 concert, which was considered by many to be his worst concert ever. He had slurred his words, forgotten lyrics, and spoken incoherently. He had several tabs open, and Jenna noted that this man apparently learned very fast. Wordlessly he clicked another tab and pulled up several different pictures of Lisa and Priscilla throughout the years. He clicked another and Jenna saw he'd watched a clip of Lisa interviewing with Oprah, and one with one of her music videos. She saw one with his grandchildren's pictures. He opened his mouth to speak, but could not for a moment. He was overcome.

Jenna gently placed her hand on his shoulder and he reached up and held it tightly. Her eyes stung with empathy—he must be devastated. At last, when he had some control of his voice, he said, "I still can't believe this. That's really me, isn't it? That's *me*, right there. I can see that...that's my face, my voice. That's me. But I can't... God... Look at me. *Look* at me!" he almost shouted, motioning to the screen. Then he clicked another tab. "And look at Lisa! She's the most perfect, beautiful thing I've ever seen in my life! And that..." He clicked back to the paused video. "...*that* is the last memory I gave her? *That's* the image she has of her father? What she carried of me into adulthood? My beautiful little girl?! I feel sick."

He stood up and went over to the balcony door. The clouds had returned, and it was another chilly day. Elvis stared into the distance, anguish still on his face. Jenna had no idea how to help as she went to stand near him. What could she possibly say? He had to face and go through this, she knew, but it was wrenching to watch.

He continued, "I mean, what kind of jackass does that when there's a little child involved? What was I thinking? She's just a little girl! She's a little baby! My little..." His eyes filled again, his face clouded with regret and pain. He crossed his arms in front of him, making him look like a lost, dejected little boy.

Instinctively, Jenna reached for his arm to offer some sort of comfort. He grabbed her and pulled her to him in a hug. He held her close and tightly, and while surprised and taken off guard, she understood his need for some level of comfort. He was seeking something, anything to dull the pain. Her ear against his chest, she could hear the internal battle to get his emotions in check.

"I am… I am *disgusted*," he said over her head. "I almost can't… God, I'm a terrible person."

"No," said Jenna, pulling back to look up at him. "Oh, no. You're not. Not at all." She looked into his haunted eyes. She took his hand and led him to the window bench. He followed like an obedient child. They sat and she turned herself to face him, looking into his eyes fiercely.

"Elvis, I need you to hear this. I mean I need you to *really* hear this." He nodded and looked down at his hands. She took both his hands in hers, inhaled deeply, and spoke.

"We know far more about addiction nowadays than back then. Your dependence on pills to function and keep yourself upright isn't a weakness, or some sort of character flaw. It's an illness, and it can be treated. It can be controlled and treated. But you aren't a bad person because you're dependent on drugs." She bent down and peered upwards into his face. He looked at her, and she thought he might cry in earnest. She'd never seen a person look that miserable. "You're arguably the greatest entertainer that ever lived, but you're a man. Just a man, m'dear. You're a flesh and blood, heart-beating-in-your-chest, human man. You're subject to the same flaws and defects as everyone else." He nodded and wiped his eyes, still not speaking. "And guess what? You got given another chance. You have what not a single other person I've ever heard of has gotten— you're being given one shot to change it *all*. Everything from this moment on. You get to rewrite history for yourself. And by rewriting *your* history, you will also rewrite it for your family, your friends, and presumably the whole world. That includes Lisa. Gawd, do you know what millions of others would give for this chance? To be able to go back and undo mistakes? Make different choices? Choose different paths? Holy shit—look at this *gift* you've been given!" He raised his head and met her gaze, less anguish on his face. "And also, you need to know that Lisa's memories are not of you as an addict. She has stated many times she knew you were ill, she worried about you a lot, but that you were a doting, loving father to her. She carried *that* into adulthood too, Elvis. She knew very clearly that you loved her. So now, yes, look at the pictures. Read the articles. Watch the videos. Learn from it. Don't look away, even though it hurts. *See* what's coming so you can best form a plan of attack." She took his face in her hands. "Then. *Change. It.*" He put both his hands over hers and nodded determinedly. Then he got up and went back to the laptop.

Jenna left him to his thoughts as he processed his feelings and newfound knowledge. She stared out the window and wondered how quickly she'd be committed if she ever tried to tell this story.

After about 30 minutes of quiet, with Jenna stealing quick glances at his progress, Elvis clapped and stood up abruptly. He rubbed his face and looked at Jenna.'

"I'm ready. I want to see the house."

"The pictures weren't enough? It's a museum now, Elvis."

"I know. I just want to drive by. Or can we go in?"

"We'd have to buy tickets."

"It's *my* house," he said, an edge of irritation creeping into his voice.

"It *was* your house. Now it's Lisa's and she lets everyone have a little bit of it."

He sighed and walked over to her. "I still want to see it."

Jenna sighed. How was she going to pull *this* off? Certainly no one expected to be seeing a man 45 years dead, but there was *no* mistaking who this man was.

"You'd have to disguise yourself somehow. We can't have you recognized."

"Why? No one would actually think it's me, right?"

"Maybe not initially, but you're pretty unmistakably you. Eventually someone is going to figure it out." Jenna went to the coat closet and pulled out a small tub.

"I think I have…" she murmured as she rummaged in the tub. "Yes! Here it is!" she exclaimed with a grin. She held out a gray hat with an applique heart and long ear flaps. "This'll help."

Elvis came over and took the hat. "You're kidding. "

"Well, you have to cover up those fender-sized sideburns somehow. Either that or go trim them down to normal human size," she said, hands on her hips.

He looked wounded. "Fender-sized? What's that supposed to mean?"

"I mean exactly that. They're sort of reasonable now, I guess, but still too big. And later they're just silly, even for the 70s. You watched that video last night. You saw them."

He looked at the hat then back at her.

"Either way, you're probably going to need to wear the hat. Or at least some sort of hat. And we'll get you some sunglasses.

"I'm not wearing this hat."

"Then go trim down those ginormous sideburns."

"Ginormous?"

"Yes." She laughed and his eyes danced with amusement.

"Okay," he said, playfully throwing the hat at her and heading into the bathroom.

She heard water running. He emerged after about ten minutes, grinning from ear to ear.

"Okay, they're trimmed."

Jenna laughed out loud and nodded, deciding not to make fun of the half-inch of white skin patches he had just exposed. He walked over the table where she'd set the hat and put it on, pretending to pout.

Jenna laughed again and handed him the shoes from the duffel. She pulled on a heavy sweater, grabbed her keys and purse, tossed him some sunglasses, and they left the apartment.

"What's that?" Elvis asked, pointing to a round button on the dash.

Jenna smiled and pushed it, starting the car. He was wide-eyed, but said nothing as he scanned the dash and controls. He was completely awed by the backup camera.

"Watch this," Jenna said. "Siri, navigate to Graceland."

Siri responded and a map appeared on her car screen. Elvis' eyes popped. "Cool, huh?"

"Yeah. That is really cool," he said, now touching the dash and various knobs.

They pulled out of the parking lot after several demonstrations of the back hatch door opening and closing, and a short argument about whether he was going to wear his seatbelt, and got onto Highway 240. His eyes were glued to the map as he watched their progress for a while, then he sat silently, looking pensively out the window. His hat and sunglasses didn't disguise even a tiny portion of who he was to her eye, but hopefully to others, who wouldn't be looking for him, it would be enough. She wasn't dumb enough to believe he wouldn't insist on going in, which would put him in close quarters with lots of people getting very up close views of this man.

Eventually they were turning off Elvis Presley Boulevard into the Graceland parking lot. As they passed by the stone wall, Elvis turned and craned his neck to see the house. She turned off the engine and waited. He was quiet for a moment.

"I have to see it. And I *have* to see that airplane."

Jenna nodded. "I know you do. I guess we'll have to risk it."

Tickets bought, they got in the queue for the shuttle. Elvis was nervous and kept pacing as they waited in line, with nowhere to put his constant reserve of restlessness. Finally they boarded the shuttle and he turned to stare at the *Lisa Marie* airplane as long as he could. They rode through the gates of Graceland, and as they drove up the long driveway, she tried to read his face, but his expression was inscrutable. It remained so mostly through the house and Vernon's office, though he was clearly a mixture of amused and baffled as they stared at the Jungle Room. He looked questioningly at her as he motioned at the room and she shrugged.

"Elvis had pretty famously bad taste about some things," she said, smiling. He shot her a look of annoyance, then reset his face to blank as they walked to the meditation garden. He saw the graves and his jaw set, his breath quickened. They followed the line of people around the circle as he gazed at the graves of his mother, father, grandmother, and his own. She saw his eyes flicker up to the tomb of Lisa's son, and she saw pain flash on his face. Jenna was about to whisper a brief explanation, but he cut her off, saying, "I know. I saw it last night." He walked over to it and stood, solemn and grieving for a grandchild he did not know, for a beloved daughter he only knew as a baby. Jenna sat on the riser steps by the columns, prepared to wait as long as he needed to stand there.

He was quiet on the drive down the street to the Walgreen's, but did shoot her a look when she suggested he wait in the car. He trailed around the store behind her as she collected a toothbrush, comb, and a few other things for him. He was clearly distracted and a million miles away as Jenna noticed the cashier looking intently at him. Elvis was completely oblivious. Finally, as Jenna paid and was feeling increasingly nervous, the cashier spoke.

"Do you work here in Memphis?" Elvis didn't respond—he was still off somewhere in his thoughts.

"Sir?"

"Oh, beg pardon. What did you say?"

"Do you work here in Memphis?" she asked again, peering very closely at his face.

"Uh, yeah, periodically," he answered without thinking. "Usually LA or Nashville."

"Oh. Well, you must be pretty good. You sure look like him." She smiled.

"Do I?" he asked, realizing what was happening and also feeling immediately uncomfortable.

Jenna smiled and put her wallet away as she picked up the bag. "Yes, he's absolutely the *best* Elvis."

She ushered them both out the door. "Super. Just couldn't wait ten minutes in the car, could you?" She glowered at him.

Later Elvis sat perched on the bar chair, looking into the kitchen as Jenna made dinner. Hamburgers sizzled while she turned frozen french fries and sliced a tomato.

"Do you have a Bible?" he asked.

Looking up from her cutting board, Jenna said, "A Bible? Yes. Second shelf by the Edgar Allen Poe." She motioned vaguely toward the bookcase by the dining table. He went to retrieve it, then sat down on the window bench with it, and began to read. Jenna continued to finish up dinner. She was placing the cheese on the burgers when he called into the kitchen, "This Bible hasn't been read much."

"Nope," she acknowledged.

"Aren't you a Christian?"

Jenna came in and placed the ketchup on the coffee table. She looked at him and sighed. "I suppose if I had to choose something to identify as, that'd be it."

He got up and resumed his position at the breakfast bar.

"You're an atheist, then."

"No, I believe in God."

"But you aren't a Christian?"

"Not really. I don't care for the rampant hypocrisy I see among 'religious people,'" she said, using air quotes. "And plus, I don't really need a book to tell me how to not be a jackass."

"But your relationship with God…" he began, earnest expression on his face.

"Is *my* business," she said, cutting him off. "Look—you be as religious as you want. It's cool with me. I don't care at *all*. I feel like, whatever brings you comfort, go for it. I just do not want a 'You should be religious and here's why' lecture, from you or anyone else. Okay?"

She put two cheeseburgers on buns then slid them onto two plates, fries next to the burgers, cold Pepsis opened. She pushed his plate across the countertop to him and came out to sit down.

"Besides, cherry-picking parts of any religious doctrine isn't what I'm interested in."

"Cherry-picking? What do you mean?" he asked, sitting beside her and reaching for the ketchup.

"I mean choosing which parts of a religion to adhere to and disregarding the parts that are less convenient."

"Are you saying I do that?" He looked absolutely scandalized.

"I'm saying everyone does it, and yes, that includes you."

"I don't! I don't at all. I try to follow…"

Jenna put her hand up to cut him off again. "Tell me aaalll about that Bible you're reading and what it says about adultery, hmm? You *are* married, are you not?" She looked him square in the face and didn't flinch. His mouth was open and he looked like he'd just eaten something sour.

"I agreed to do this because I believe you need a second chance. I believe you're too important to the world to not try this. I'm just a teacher—a nobody. You really *matter*. But I will *not* have a religious discussion or debate with you. Full. Stop." Her gaze lingered in his eyes another moment, then she picked up the remote and turned on Netflix. She ate her burger in silence, and so did he.

Settled into the window seat with her Elvis pillow and a book, Jenna disengaged from Elvis for the rest of the evening. He remained on the couch, though she had no idea if he was watching TV or dozing. He had his books about himself nearby and she thought he was thumbing through them periodically. She stretched and glanced at her phone to check the time: 10:20. She'd been sitting here in her own little world for almost three hours. Returning to her book, she contemplated going to bed when she was suddenly aware that he was standing by the window seat. She hadn't heard him get up or walk over. He sat down at the opposite end of the bench, stretched his legs out, his feet against her hip and her feet against his. As he adjusted a pillow behind him, she looked carefully at his face. He was, hands-down, the most beautiful human she'd ever seen. It almost defied the imagination that someone could actually be that handsome. She pulled a purple afghan throw over both their legs and put her book to the side. When she looked up, he was watching her intently.

"You don't like me much, do you? I mean, you don't think much of me as a person." He said the last sentence not as a question, but as a statement of fact. He searched her face, an anxiousness in his eyes.

"What? Don't like you? Where did you get that from?"

Elvis looked down and started picking at the throw blanket. "The pills. The crack about adultery."

He glanced up at her quickly, then back down. "The whole I mess I made, or, I guess, will make, of stuff. How I left Daddy and 'Cilla with no money for Lisa or for the house."

"God, Elvis, no," Jenna said earnestly. "I don't dislike you at all. I think the absolute world of you. I always have."

He looked up again, hesitantly. Jenna went on. "I'm not a fan of some of your choices, sure, but jeez—no. I like you quite well. And I think well *of* you." She grinned mischievously. "Especially with the added attraction of two white patches on your face."

He put both hands up to the little bald patches and laughed. He looked toward the window, laughter fading. He stared a moment, and without moving his gaze he said, "I'm so alone. There's just so much other people don't get. Don't know. I get so tired sometimes. And I can't sleep hardly at all. And there's stuff I want to do. Things I want to do, you know, professionally. Places I want to go. And I can't." He looked at her again, then down at his hands. "And I can't explain why I am telling you all of this. Mostly I've never said these things out loud to anyone."

Tears stung Jenna's eyes and she took his hand. "I know. I wish I could help. I wish… I would do something about all of that if I could. I'd—"

"You are," he broke in. "You're actually helping me a lot. You're telling me things I don't want to hear. I hate it, but I know it's helping me. I know because you're mostly right. And I *hate* that I have to admit you're right. And I can't exactly escape, can I? Where the hell would I go?" He smiled a little. "Plus, like I said, I have this weird sense, like I can say things here and not be embarrassed or have you think…"

"You can say whatever you want to me. I am here to hear you. And, you're right, you're a captive audience," Jenna acknowledged.

"I…I just… I don't know why. Why me? Why am I here and why was *I* picked for this?"

"Picked for what? The second chance or just being Elvis at all?"

"Either. Both. I don't know." He shrugged.

Jenna leaned back, releasing his hand. "I'm going to say to you the same thing I tell my students every semester about you. You changed the world. Period. You *literally* changed the world. At least the Western world. No, you did, Elvis," she said as he rolled his eyes. "You changed how we think, how we dress. You crossed racial lines. You changed how we talk about sex. You changed *that* we talk about sex. Like, at all. You changed what music is 'acceptable.' You changed *all* of it. Western society changed because of you, and you alone. You kicked open doors and smashed down barriers *that are still open*! Everyone who came after you had the freedoms you created for them. They walked through doors *you* opened. *You* did this. By yourself, with no map, no previous experience to pull on. Just winging it alone." He made a small, derisive snort and chuckled.

"Laugh if you want, but it's all true. So here's this guy, this very young guy, staring us, as a society, in the face with all our prejudices and our 'proper,' long-held behaviors and beliefs, and he's saying, 'No, we don't have to live inside this ridiculous little box anymore. We can kick open the doors, smash the damned box, and just...*be*. We can dance and sing and rock ourselves silly and still be decent people.'"

He nodded slightly, listening as he loosened a thread on the throw and began twisting it.

"So we rocked and we rolled and we embraced this wild new freedom. And we lauded and worshipped the man who delivered us from safe, pearl-wearing ballads and the chaste crooning of the '40s and early '50s. As a reward for this epic deliverance, we showered this young guy with money and adulation. We called him a king, and because everyone wants a piece of a king, we then drove him into his house for his own safety, and eventually into bottle after bottle of pills." Jenna reached out again as his face clouded and he looked ashamedly back at his twisted thread.

"No, don't misunderstand. You weren't the first and you damn sure aren't the last, trust me on that one. Seems as though addiction is a standard price paid for fame. But here's where you diverge from the rest: Your accomplishments and ongoing influence were and are so extraordinary that you've been given a chance to fix the bad choices. As to why you? I can't answer that. Right place, right time? I simply don't know. But you arrived with the talent, the drive, the looks, and the ability to create this absolute tsunami of change. Why it was you and not someone else, I can't say."

She peered into his face, hoping for a response. When she saw none, she continued. "So no, I don't like some of the decisions you've made. I don't like your view of women that you seem to have, and the drugs. I don't like some of the paths you've taken. But I like *you*. You're a great guy, Elvis. You're funny, and warm, and great company!"

His head snapped up. "But aren't we all the sum total of our choices? Don't the choices I make create…sum up who I am? *What* I am?"

"Yes, to an extent. We are indeed the sum of our choices. The beauty of that is that we can all choose different paths and courses of action, thereby changing the sum. At any moment of any day of any week, any of us can decide on a different course. Everyone has that freedom. For you, that freedom vanished after 1977 until yesterday. Now you have it again."

Elvis nodded and went back to worrying his pulled thread, now at least three inches long. After a long silence, he looked up into Jenna's face. "Okay, since you were clearly also 'chosen' for this, tell me: choose three things, if you were me, that you'd change right away."

"Umm… Let's see. No more pills, first thing. At least none that aren't regulated by a doctor. I'd follow a strict protocol and go into a rehab center to get off them if I have to."

He nodded and looked away, a pained expression on his face. "I don't know if I can."

"I do. You can," she said firmly. "If it means enough, you can."

"Okay, what's the second thing?"

"Wow. Umm. Let me think."

"Lord, is there *that* much to choose from?" he exclaimed, slightly outraged.

Jenna laughed. "Well, there *are* a few, and you limited me to three." They both laughed. "I think the next thing would maybe be the Colonel. And your professional life. Your own say-so in your career."

"The Colonel hasn't let me down yet. The bookings, the money—keep rolling in," he said. "And this whole International Hotel thing I'm doing now…it's been great so far."

"True, but think about the movies, for example. Would you have refused to do any of those? Said nope and just refused to sign on?"

"*Oh* yeah."

"So maybe keep him more…in check? Maybe stop the 'I just let him handle it' mindset? It's *your* career, so maybe get a solid entertainment lawyer that works solely for you? To read all this stuff he has you sign? Maybe take a more active role in what you do? Just an idea. Elvis, you have the right to say no. And also…" She put her hands up. "…Just my opinion, but there's no law that says you have to be the star of everything you do professionally. If there's something that you would enjoy or would scratch your creative itch, why not do it? If it would be fun? Or satisfying? The Colonel doesn't *have* to package and sell you any way that doesn't fit with what *you* want. Just my two cents."

He thought about this for a long moment, then gave a barely noticeable nod. "And third?"

"Probably third would be to suggest you drag yourself out of the dark ages where women are concerned. At least women you're involved with."

Elvis looked incensed. "If you're talking about Priscilla, I give her everything she could want."

"Mmm-hmm, yeah. Except a faithful husband."

Elvis looked like she'd reached out and slapped him in the mouth. "You don't know anything about that," he hissed at her.

"No, I don't. And because I don't, I'll say only this: It's well known for all of posterity that you are… shall we say…monogamy challenged? You're a serial cheater, Elvis, and I can show you book after book after article to prove it, if you don't believe me. And while all that is absolutely your choice, and absolutely between you and your wife, it goes back to the choices we've mentioned. I realize you can love your wife very much while you're with someone else. But is that the behavior you were raised with? Is that something your mom would brag about—the constant parade of women? Is that a value she'd be proud of? Is that going to sustain you? Is that how you were raised? Just something to consider." Jenna knew she was in dangerous territory and exited as fast as she could.

Neither spoke for a long time. She could see him quietly mulling things over and thinking things through as the pulled thread increased to at least six inches, and he began tying tiny knots in it as he thought. Finally he looked at her.

"What should we do next?"

"Well, I don't actually know. This is unchartered territory."

"Do you think I should go back? What if it doesn't work? What if I'm stuck here?"

"I don't know. As I said, I don't know what I'm doing any more than you do," she said. Elvis looked anxious.

"Tell you what. I'm beat. Why don't we sleep then talk about it more tomorrow?"

"That's another thing. Are we running out of time?"

"Well, they said three or so days. Tomorrow is day three. So probably, yeah."

"And if I don't go back after tomorrow, what happens?"

"Don't know that either," Jenna said, shrugging. She got up and went to the bathroom to brush her teeth. When she came back out, Elvis was on the balcony smoking a cigar.

"Was that in the bag?" she asked, opening the door.

"Yeah, they were in the bottom, under the clothes."

"Okay. I'm going to bed."

"All right. I'm going to stay out here a while. I need to think. I also want to read some more of these books. I'll just lie on the couch if I get tired later." Jenna noticed he had a different one tucked under his arm, the book written at the end of his life called *Elvis: What Happened?* She paused for a moment, wondering if she should prepare him for the fact that it was a sordid tell-all written by two people he currently trusted implicitly. She decided to just let him read it, and if he wanted to discuss it tomorrow, they would. Her heart sank as she stepped through the door. Jenna hated that book, and the very public airing of his personal life was going to hurt him deeply. Jenna wondered if he would end up absolutely hating her. This short stay with her had, so far, caused him nothing but pain and anguish.

Sometime in the dark, early hours of the morning, Jenna felt him slide into the bed with her and take her hand. He didn't touch any other part of her, and in fact seemed to be taking pains to not to be too close to her. As she drifted back into sleep, her hand in his, it occurred to her that it sounded like he'd been crying.

7

Jenna awoke to a clear morning. Sun streamed in her bedroom window as she sat up. When she didn't see Elvis, she got out of bed and pulled on her robe. Somehow not having her eyes on him made her very nervous. As she reached for the door, she heard a quiet humming and a few guitar chords. He'd opened the guitar Chris and Bill had left.

He was sitting on the window bench, absently humming what might have been "I'm So Lonesome I Could Cry" while strumming lightly.

"Morning," he said, smiling a little. To Jenna he looked sad and worn down, like a thousand-pound weight sat on his shoulders.

"Hi," she said, sitting on the couch. He stopped playing and looked at her.

"I slept for four hours," he said almost proudly. When her raised eyebrows asked why this was of importance, he reached into the bag and pulled out a pill bottle.

"Only one," he said. "I only needed one." He tossed the bottle back into the bag. "Seems like there's been something different since…since, you know, I got here."

"Different?"

"Yeah, like maybe something changed in here." He patted his chest and abdomen. "With all that spinning and twisting and shit."

"Well, certainly could have. I don't know," Jenna said. "Hey, I have a thought."

"What?"

"Let's go to the park."

"The park? Why?"

"Well, news flash: not everyone lives like a bat. Some of us like sunshine."

He rolled his eyes and picked the guitar back up, strumming lightly again. "Fine by me—I have my disguise."

Jenna went to the kitchen and got cereal and toast started. After a quick meal, she went to put on clean clothes. She rebraided her hair down her back pulled on her tennis shoes, and grabbed a jacket. She found him on the balcony again, smoking another cigar. He looked sideways at her, impish grin on his face.

"Live like a bat," he said, chuckling.

She clicked the lock on her car and the *beep-beep* made Elvis look back at it with interest. He turned to the wide, asphalt pathway before them. They had seen a row of crafters and flea market sellers set up on their way into the park and had agreed to find them.

Elvis grinned a silly, boyish grin and stuck out his elbow at her to offer his arm.

"M'lady?"

Jenna put her hand through his arm with an exaggerated sweep. "Many thanks, kind sir."

Laughing, they stayed arm in arm, walking in step together. His gray hat was pulled down over his ears, the ear flaps hanging past his chin. The sunglasses were mirrored black. They strolled in amiable silence, Elvis humming periodically. His face looked relatively relaxed for the first time since technology had landed him on her bedroom floor.

"There's a certain safety here," he said, still looking ahead down the path.

"Safety? What do you mean?"

"Well, when I landed ass-first on the floor, I was angry and pretty confused. Disoriented. Kind of freaked out." He leaned over and smiled. "Saw that on a video last night." He laughed. "But I had to come to terms with it as being real because there was no denying the physical proof. I had experienced something crazy. Something completely out there. Just like when you showed me the pictures and videos of me in '77. I have eyes—I saw absolutely that was me. The voice was me. The face was me. So I had to accept quickly that even though it's completely nuts, it's true. It's happening." He looked down at Jenna and she nodded. "Then there was you, telling me things that would have gotten anyone else's ass kicked. I still don't want to hear some of what you keep saying. The only thing that keeps me here is the videos and the pictures—the proof. I just cannot deny this is actually real."

"Well, that and the fact that you don't really exist and can't actually go anywhere."

"Well, yeah, and that. But as long as I've had you telling me about myself, and showing me crap I don't want to see, don't want to know, I haven't had to make decisions. I haven't had to *do* anything. But I was thinking about that this morning before you got up. I think that I do now. I need to go back and make some decisions. And I'm not sure I can. It's safer here, maybe *because* I don't exist. I've even had a couple of moments where I wondered if I could just stay here. Just *poof*." His face had gone serious and was troubled. He sighed. "I think I could stay for a long time. I keep thinking what if I could stay here with you and get to go anywhere I want, any time I want, and not have to think about anything."

Jenna hugged his arm tightly to her and laid her head on his upper arm for a moment before she spoke, relieved that he didn't appear to harbor any ill will toward her for this whole odyssey. "I can't imagine how frightening the tasks ahead of you are. I've never been famous. I've never had people relying on me for their income. But this I *do* know: You've already changed the whole round world. So you sure as shit can change just you."

He was quiet a moment then said, "I wonder if that's what I've been searching for all this time."

"What is?"

"That maybe I've known what my purpose is all along. I think I knew it more clearly at 19 than I do now. I have to wonder if it was simply to do what I'm doing—music. Showing people what they have in common, bringing people together from everywhere to sing and dance and have fun, if only for a little while."

"There's probably no better purpose on earth. Elvis the uniter." Jenna laughed. He smiled as they strolled on.

"Where did you get to be so no-nonsense?" he asked. "Man, you can lay something open to the *bone*."

"Eh. Who knows? I'm hard-wired with a low bullshit tolerance. Maybe my Nan's influence."

"Bullshit tolerance. That's great!" He laughed out loud, then said, "I seem to dish out plenty of that."

"Everyone does. You're not special there, hun. What's unusual in your case, what's different from regular people, is that you lost your crap-o-meter when your mom died. I think she maybe was an accurate gauge, and since then, you've had no one to tell you you're being stupid, like the rest of us have. And if I'm understanding Elvis 'The Legend,' even when they tell you you're being stupid, you aren't interested—and always know better."

Jenna was on edge at having made this last comment, fearing his reaction. But she was running out of time, so she decided to say it.

He was quiet a moment, then he snorted and chuckled. "I need to buy everyone in my life a crap-o-meter and make it sound a little buzzer at me. Then I'll have a little slice of your face to keep me in line." He smiled. "Where can I buy a large number of crap-o-meters?"

"Somewhere between 1969 and 2022, I guess." Jenna laughed.

They smiled at each other as they approached the first art table. They looked at books, paintings, woodworking. Elvis was clearly enamored with an intricately carved wooden pistol. Jenna rolled her eyes.

"What?" he said, putting it back and following her to the next table.

"Your preoccupation with guns is strange," she said, fingering some silver jewelry.

"It is not. What's wrong with guns? They're cool," he protested, hands on his hips.

"Uh-huh. Lots of things are cool till you have a gazillion of them. Then it's weird."

He huffed, but didn't respond. His attention fell on a collection of sterling silver animal jewelry. His eyes trailed over foxes and bears, cats and dogs, then fell on an owl set. He picked up the box with an owl ring and pendant.

"This is nice. Let's get these."

"An owl?"

"Yeah. I'll wear the pendant as a reminder for my crap-o-meter. You can be my wise old owl." He laughed, but his eyes didn't sparkle. They looked preoccupied and worried.

"Okay. I'll take the ring. Maybe when you're about to do something stupid the owl can peck you or something." Jenna marveled at her inherent desire to make this man happy. It was such a strange phenomenon—almost a compulsion. *What is it about him?*

He smiled and said to the artist, "How much for the set?"

"Forty dollars," was the answer. The artist, a 40-something woman with long, bushy black hair peppered with gray, was peering at him strangely. Elvis sensed this immediately and pushed the sunglasses up to cover his eyes. Jenna could see that he was alert, but would not be deterred. He reached into his pants pocket and pulled out a $50 bill.

"I'll give you $50 and you swap the chain for a men's size, okay?"

"Deal," said the artist, taking the box, her gaze lingering on his face. Jenna was starting to feel uncomfortable. This person was looking at him too closely. Maybe this was a bad idea, coming out. Just as she was feeling the need to leave, the woman returned with the box, closed it, and took the bill Elvis handed her. She looked intently at his right hand, then said, "You know, you look astoundingly like Elvis. Like, he could be your brother."

"Huh," Elvis said. "No, I usually hear that I look like Engelbert Humperdinck," he shot back with a grin.

"Who?" she called, but they were already walking away. Elvis laughed out loud, and Jenna joined him.

"I guess if I slapped you or something, it wouldn't help?"

"Not a bit."

"Where did you get $50?"

"It was in my pants pocket. Seems like I remember putting it in there a while back, but I can't say for sure."

They walked in silence, heading back to the car, Jenna wondering when the artist would realize she accepted a bill from the 1960's.

As they walked through the door of the apartment, Jenna's phone buzzed with an incoming text. She took her phone out and opened the message. Her face clouded, so Elvis stopped after he closed the door.

"What?"

"A text. From Chris," she said, handing him the phone. Elvis read it aloud.

"Did not mention before—do not allow Elvis near any travel where he would encounter himself. This is not an explored area."

He handed the phone back to her. "What does this mean?"

Jenna was sitting on the couch, twisting her owl ring. He came and sat by her, removing the hat and glasses.

"It means, I think, that if we jump into a time where you already are, now-you can't be seen by then-you."

Elvis nodded. "Okay, but were we planning to jump? I thought I was just going back."

Jenna started to text, then hit Send. "This morning I sent an inquiry text about if we could jump back to where you hit your head so hard."

"Why?"

"To prevent it? Duh?"

The phone vibrated again, and Jenna opened it, reading aloud.

"Yes, going to the time is okay. But Elvis cannot see himself."

Jena texted her thanks and went over to the window bench. "This makes the plan I was thinking of tricky," she said.

"Plan?"

"Yeah. Since you need to go back tonight, I thought we could go together to somehow stop that terrible fall and head injury. If there's anything to the theory that that had a connection to your immune system problems, why not remove it from the equation? I was hoping to have you with me to find the location more easily."

He nodded. "Well, we still can, can't we?"

"Maybe, but it's pretty risky. You seeing yourself would apparently be a bad idea. It's probably also a bad idea to have anyone who knew you see the 1969-you in 1967."

They fell into a contemplative silence, each mulling over potential options for maximum results. Suddenly Jenna noticed he had removed his owl pendant. She made an exaggerated sad face.

"Where's your owl?"

He smiled and patted his hip. "In my pocket. I'm going to make a few improvements to it." He grinned like a little boy with a surprise.

Jenna smiled and nodded. "Okay." *That should be interesting*, she thought. He wasn't known for his dignified reserve when purchasing jewelry.

Elvis stood up, reached for a cigar, and went to the balcony. She followed him.

"Hey" she said, sitting down. "In your day, people smoked inside without a thought. How come you always come out here?"

He puffed the cigar, grinned, and said, "Because there aren't any ashtrays in there."

Jenna nodded and after a few minutes, he turned to her and said, "Let's do this then. We'll both go back to where I came from, then from there, you can go to stop the fall."

"That's fine, but us going together to Vegas where you were isn't necessary. You can go back, and I can go deal with the fall."

He looked disappointed. "I know, but I want you to. Just for a short while." He paused, then his face lit up. "We can send both messages at the same time! Then we won't have to find a phone to call in the jump! Yours can be like an hour later or something!"

"All right! You can show me around your International Hotel. Show me the 'funky angels.'" She laughed as she got up to go in. "I'll make us something to eat, then we'll decide when to text."

His smile faded as he nodded vaguely, and she felt a strange hollowness. Their bizarre journey was nearly over. He'd been here such a short time. She would miss him immeasurably: his company, his smile. She blinked hard and went to make some lunch.

A half hour later they were in their respective positions on the window bench, eating hot grilled cheese sandwiches and potato chips. Jenna wiped her fingers with a napkin and looked at his face. He was chewing, looking out at the distant trees.

"I don't know if I can do this all this by myself," he said, not shifting his stare.

"I do. I know. You can. You can accomplish anything you set out to do."

He took another bite of sandwich, but looked a little forlorn. "I know it seems daunting," she said, "but I have absolute faith in you. And you don't have to do anything by yourself. You have a wife who loves you and an entire support system to pull on. Ask them to support you. Tell them you need this. Let them help you."

His gaze met hers for a moment. He swallowed his bite and reached for the bag of chips. "I'm glad one of us has faith in me. Because, man, I don't."

They finished eating and set aside their plates, then remained on the bench, lost in thought.

"Oh, also," Jenna said. "Start taking vitamin D."

"Okay... Why?" he asked, a chuckle on his lips.

"Because, as previously discussed, you live like a bat."

"A bat. Yes...vitamin D?"

"It's now known that it helps with immune system function. You are *never* in the sun. Just try it. It can't hurt, can it?"

"Don't suppose it can."

"Oh, and before I forget, there's something I've been meaning to mention and I keep forgetting," she said.

His eyebrows raised. "What?"

"In 1973, Dolly Parton wrote a song called 'I Will Always Love You.'"

"Who? Why is that name vaguely familiar?"

"Because she's a freaking *legend*, that's why. Anyway, she wrote what is one of the most beautiful love songs of the 20th century, and asked *you* to sing it."

"Okay..."

"The Colonel said no."

Elvis' jaw tightened. "I make those decisions. Not him."

"Yeah, well, he insisted on half the publishing rights and she said no to that."

"That's kind of standard for our deals."

"Well, stop it. It was *her* song. You missed out on an absolutely wonderful song and you made Dolly cry. Shame on you. No one should make Dolly Parton cry."

"I... What? You're scolding me for something I haven't done yet?"

"Well, don't do it when the time arrives. Or ever. I can't imagine the songs you're missing out on because the Colonel wants more money. That's what I mean when I said you need to steer your own professional decisions more."

Elvis smiled. "I'll keep it in mind."

"Good," she said, still disgruntled.

After another silence, he looked at her and said, "I need you to know you're not 'just a teacher,' and that you're one *hell* of a lady." He looked sheepish and uncomfortable, but his eyes were sincere and shining.

Jenna welled up and took his hand. "Thank you. And I need *you* to know you're not just a singer or entertainer. You're more than what you do for a living. You're a flesh-and-blood man. You have a wife and a baby. You can steer your own life, and you can learn to ask for help from those who love you. Get a say-so in your career. Well, more of one. Invest money to save for Lisa. Get a lawyer for only yourself and *your* interests, and your family's interests." Elvis nodded.

"I'm going to miss you like crazy, Elvis."

He nodded, obviously emotional. "Me too," he said.

Then he sighed and stood up. "But we don't have to do all that right now." He smiled a huge grin. "Get your phone. Let's go to Vegas!"

8

The text was sent, and the response said 3 to 5 minutes would be their timeframe. She'd sent two carefully constructed texts, one to send them both back to '69 at the International on the date he came from, and one about an hour later to send just her to '67 at his home on Rocca Place in Bel Air, then her back home about half an hour later. They debated about whether 30 minutes would be enough time for her to accomplish her task, but he insisted the house simply wasn't *that* big and certainly that would be sufficient.

When they had loaded the duffel bag, he placed it over his shoulder and clutched the handle of his guitar case tightly. Jenna had her front door key, her license, and $20 and some change in her pocket. She chose to leave her purse and phone in the apartment. They stood together, hugging as tightly as they could, eyes squeezed shut in anticipation of the patently unpleasant experience ahead. She could hear his heart pounding and both of them were breathing like they'd run a marathon.

The tingle started in her leg and she squeezed him tighter. She felt him tense up and suck in his breath, then the spinning sensation began. The unseen force shoved them from behind, more spinning and pins and needles, then they both crashed onto a very hard concrete floor. The guitar clattered to the floor loudly and Elvis was muttering profanity.

"Who's there?" came a voice from behind a door. Elvis jumped up first, reeled sideways trying to right his balance, and grabbed the guitar and duffel. Jenna staggered to her feet and they both scuttled behind a partition covered in carpeting, clearly a large size to separate a whole room. They heard a very nearby door open and they both froze.

"Someone in here?"

They stayed as quiet as they could, though Jenna was certain her thundering pulse would give them away. The door closed after a moment and they heard footsteps walking away. Elvis sagged against the concrete wall and Jenna plopped onto a stack of wooden pallets. His breathing was ragged and he wiped sweat off his face.

"Damn, that is *awful*. I *hate* that shit," he said, to himself more than to Jenna.

Nodding, Jenna got to her feet carefully, holding her balance on the palettes. "Agreed."

After a few more minutes of collecting themselves, they gathered the guitar and duffel and crept to the door.

"Where's the elevator?" Jenna whispered.

"No idea. Never been down here," he whispered back. "But this is the door the guy was in, so it has to lead somewhere."

"I guess it wouldn't be a disaster to be seen. This is where you jumped from, after all—you belong here."

"Yeah, but I don't want to have to explain why I'm in the basement with a duffel bag and a guitar, looking like I'm running away from home, and with some strange girl."

Jenna shot him a look and he laughed quietly. They crept down the hallway, listening carefully, both of them still slightly dizzy and queasy. A few more corridors led them to a large service elevator, which they took to the backstage area. They could hear people milling about, but no one near enough to spot them. Elvis pushed open a black metal door and led her through, her holding his hand in the dark.

"It's so dark in here I can't see anything," she whispered, tiptoeing in tiny steps so she wouldn't fall over something.

"Yeah, hang on," he said. They reached a dark curtain and he groped around till it parted, and he pulled them both through. Jenna sucked in her breath as her eyes adjusted to the dim lighting. She could see they were standing on a massive stage, and the audience seating was enormous—sloping upwards for what seemed like miles.

"This is… This is the stage, isn't it?" she breathed, completely awestruck.

Elvis grinned a wide smile and splayed his arms out. "Yep! This is it! Where we do the show every night! What do you think?" He turned a complete circle, arms still extended.

"It's *wonderful!*" Jenna gushed, genuinely overcome. She was speechless as she connected the pictures she knew so well to the actual stage. "I'd give anything to see you…" She trailed off, knowing she couldn't. Time was already running short.

His smile faded as he walked over to her, sadness in his eyes. "Okay, listen. I will bring the *house* down for you tonight. I promise. You look when you get back. You'll see. I'm gonna absolutely *kill* it tonight. They'll be talking about this shit for *years*." He took his pendant out of his pocket and put it on. "It's not improved yet, but I'm wearing it tonight."

"You'll do 'My Babe?'" she asked tearfully.

"Absolutely. I'm gonna tear into that song so hard you'll feel it from 2022. For you." He smiled grimly, working to keep to his lumpy throat in check. He took her hand and sang quietly, "My babe don't stand no cheater…"

Jenna laughed. "This babe don't stand no cheater…" she sang back. They both smiled at each other.

Jenna's eyes stung and her chest felt tight. This was the end of the road—goodbye for now. Would she ever see him again? Would he live to 2022? Or would she return to her time and find he'd passed away months, or even years before? If he lived, he'd be a very old man when she returned. Had they set anything in motion to make a difference? Was he determined enough to change his life? If he did change his own destiny, if he did live past 1977, what effect would it have on his family? How would their paths and destinies change? His friends? The music industry? Even the whole world?

She walked over to the edge of the stage and stood, picturing a cheering, screaming crowd of

2,000 people watching this man do what he did better than pretty much anyone else on earth.

"I wanted you to see the stage," he said. He had walked up next to her.

"Thank you," she whispered, turning to face him. "I want you to live longer, Elvis. I want you to have a full, long life full of love and happiness and accomplishments. For you. For your family. Did this work? All of this insanity? Will you make changes for yourself? Will you let people help you? Please?"

He looked up to the top row of seating and sighed. "I'm going to try. I can't do much now until this gig is over. But after that…" He trailed off and looked misty. "Priscilla and I need to…talk."

Jenna nodded. "Yeah, I think you do," she murmured.

"And I have to look hard at some stuff. Those pictures of me…the videos… I… God, I need to…" His voice was so quiet, she could barely hear him. She tucked her arm through his and they stood quietly for a long time, each lost in thought.

"I should to go back to the basement," she finally said. "Time is almost up and I think I should be where we landed."

He nodded and walked over to get the bag and guitar. They threaded their way through the curtain and retraced their steps back to the basement, ducking out of sight only twice.

"This place is about to come alive, getting ready for the show tonight," he said.

"Yes. Good luck." she answered, her eyes filling and stinging as she took his hands.

"Promise me you'll come," he said, his voice cracking.

"I promise. I promise on my Nan I'll come. I swear on everything I hold dear that I'll come. March 10th, 2022, I'm coming to Graceland. And you'd *better* be there, alive and well."

"I'll be waiting."

"Vitamin D." She laughed, letting go of him and stepping away.

"Vitamin D," he said, smiling. His eyes glistened as he yanked her into a tight hug and he kissed her forehead. She squeezed him for all she was worth, put her hands on his face, and took his hands. They gazed at each other for a moment, then she stepped back from him.

"Jenna, thank you," he said.

"And thank *you*," she said, her leg beginning to tingle. "I'll miss you!"

"I'll be waiting for you! Don't you forget me! I need the crap-o-meter!"

Jenna laughed as the tingle spread up her body and it looked like Elvis was standing with a spotlight on him as the basement faded to black. His face became fuzzy, blurred completely, then was gone.

She landed with an unceremonious *thud* on a carpeted floor. She rolled onto her back and wished she could stop being dumped onto floors. Rubbing her elbow, she got up to her knees, but she was too dizzy to stand. She sat back down, resting her head on her arms. The lurching stopped in her stomach, so she tried to stand again. This attempt was more successful if she used the wall for balance. She looked around and realized she was in a bedroom, and had landed on the floor in front of the bathroom. She appraised her environment, listening for any sounds or sign of life. Surely she wasn't here alone. She heard absolutely nothing. What were the odds of no one being here? Her eyes took in gold carpeting, a double bed with a creamy white quilted bedspread, and dark wood dressers. She chuckled quietly to herself. "Sixties style right here," she whispered.

Mentally going over Elvis' description of where his bathroom was, she tiptoed to the door and pressed her ear against it. Quiet. Gritting her teeth, she turned the knob and eased the door open an inch. She still heard nothing. Feeling braver, she pulled the door open wide enough for her to get through, then stood silently listening again. This time she heard something. A voice? It sounded like it was outside. Damn. Someone was here. She'd set the time here in '67 for only 30 minutes. If she needed longer, she'd have to get to a landline. Her eyes darted to the number still in marker on her arm. All she had to do was wind through the labyrinth of halls and find his bathroom, cut the TV cord off, and get back to this room. Easy, right? She sighed.

Easing herself into the hallway, she tried to orient herself based on what Elvis had told her. Nothing seemed familiar. She made her way down the hall she was in, trying to make a note of which hallway it was, then scanned for any sign of the kitchen. She needed a scissors or sharp knife. She didn't want to rely on her ability to rip the cord out of the TV bare-handed. She finally stumbled onto the kitchen's location, and after scanning for anyone nearby, she started quietly searching for a pair of scissors. She had to hurry—he supposedly fell tonight, and she only had about 20 minutes left to try to prevent this from happening.

She found a sharp knife in a drawer and picked it up. Now to find his bathroom. She eased herself down another hallway, peeking in doors to find his bedroom. At last she found it. The moment she peered into the door, she knew this was it. She stepped just inside the door and closed it carefully. She saw the bathroom door and ran-walked over to it. Sure enough, there was a small television on the counter and the cord was on the floor in front of the cabinet. Swiftly she snatched up the cord and traced it all the way to the outlet, unplugged it, then found its source on the back of the TV. She started sawing the cord even with the back so that it couldn't be repaired. Of course, she knew Elvis could have it replaced with a snap of his fingers, but maybe he wouldn't until tomorrow, preventing tonight's fall and head injury.

Severed cord and the knife in hand, she turned and froze as she heard voices in the hallway. *Please don't let them come in here. Please.* Someone walked down the hall and sounded like they may have gone to the kitchen. She didn't want to risk entering the kitchen again if she could help it. She wildly looked around the room, seeking an out of the way place for the knife and cord. There was a stash of toilet paper under the sink. She was carefully and quietly laying them both inside, behind the rolls to the left, when she heard the bedroom door open. She closed the cabinet softly and stood completely still, straining to hear who had entered.

A female voice said, "Yeah, hang on. Let me put these towels in his bathroom."

Jenna felt panic. She had to hide! Where? She looked around, hysteria rising inside her, and dashed over to the bathtub and stepped in. As quietly as possible she gingerly pulled the curtain and crouched down. The bathroom door opened and she heard someone step inside. Her chest was banging with her wild heartbeat as she peered up and to her right at the edge of the long bathroom mirror. She could only see a woman's shoulder and the corner of a tall stack of white fluffy towels set onto the edge of the bathroom counter. There were small sounds that might have been straightening up items on the counter, then the water ran for a moment. Then the tap shut off, the woman sighed, and she heard her steps leave the bathroom. A moment later, she heard the bedroom door click shut.

Still riveted to the bathtub with fear, Jenna was almost panting as she willed her heart rate to slow. How much time was left? She had to get back to that bedroom—she must be almost out of time.

She stood up and pulled the curtain back, craning her neck toward the door, listening. When she heard nothing, she stepped over to the bedroom door. There was silence, so she oozed herself out into the hallway, pulling the door shut behind her.

She had to get back to the kitchen, since that was her landmark for finding that bedroom again. Just as she reached it, she heard someone entering the house. She dropped to the floor, ducking below the countertop. *Please don't let them be hungry.* The male voices (Vernon?) sounded like they turned left, away from the kitchen. She decided to chance it and crawled over to the door. When all was quiet, she stood up and scurried down the hallway to the door she'd landed in. As she closed it behind her, she heard a male voice calling after her—she'd been seen. *Damnit.* She ran to the bathroom doorway just as the tingle started in her leg. It ran up her body and the spinning sensation began to swirl. She saw the bedroom door, now appearing as though a spotlight were on it, fling open, and a man walked in, clearly yelling something that was too muffled and distorted to hear. The sensation of being shoved from behind jerked her forward and she slammed, forehead first, into her own dresser in her own apartment.

"Oooowwww," she said aloud, rolling to her back. "Jeez *Louise* with these landings!" She lay there, staring at the ceiling, sick, queasy, and utterly exhausted. Who had seen her as she jumped? That'd be a story to tell, if anyone believed him: some strange woman disappeared into thin air in Elvis' house in 1967. She chuckled.

Spinning sensation abated, so she sat up and grabbed her phone off the edge of the bed where she'd left it. March 9, 2022. She made it. She was back. And her head hurt.

With a start, she jumped up and leaned against her dresser as her stomach lurched. *Laptop.* She had to see if this had worked. She staggered into the living room, pausing to look for a moment at the window bench where they had sat together just a few hours before. Had it really only been a few hours? Before she went to her computer she walked, more steadily now, to the balcony. There were his cigar butts, right where he'd left them. She grabbed them up and held them to her, inhaling the aroma.

She searched "8/12/69 Vegas performance" first. The reviews were stunning. He had performed like a wild animal, one reporter wrote. Another said he'd never in his whole career looked or sounded better. He'd brought them to their feet again and again. Just as he'd promised, he brought the house down. She clicked a picture of him from that night. Enlarging it, she saw the owl pendant. He *had* worn it. She clicked picture after picture until her hand hurt.

In very late August of '69, she saw the pendant again—but it looked different. The owl was now sitting on a silver branch that had C-O-M engraved on it. C-O-M? She was puzzled. What... Oh my God, she thought. Crap-o-meter! She burst into tears and sobbed like a toddler, releasing days of anxiety and worry. It was over. Still sniffling and crying, she made her way to her bed, clutching the cigar butts, and collapsed into an exhausted sleep. It was over. She'd saved Elvis.

9

Lisa, eyes red and watery, with an amassed pile of tissues next to her, leaned back in her chair.

"So you cut the cord completely off to stop the fall?"

"I did. Hacked it off and hid it. I didn't know what else to do with it! I was too scared to go back to the kitchen to put the knife back, especially after I'd almost been caught." Jenna chuckled and Elvis laughed out loud.

"I found that damn thing a few days later, the knife next to it. I had no *idea* what to think at that time. I thought the house was haunted or something after Joe told me the story of the 'disappearing woman' in the bedroom."

"Oh, that was Joe?" Jenna asked.

"No, it was a gardener who had come in for some water. He saw you going down the hall and knew you didn't belong there. He thought a fan had gotten in. He told Joe, who told me."

The three of them sat in silence for a moment, then Lisa leaned toward Jenna, her eyes glittering and intense.

"Thank you for saving my father."

"You're welcome. But I didn't save him. *He* saved him," Jenna said, her voice cracking. She reached out and put her hand on Elvis' arm. "*He* did the work.

He did what he needed to do. All I did was show him what was coming if he didn't change his ways."

"Like some weird ghost of Elvis' future," Elvis said, laughing. "I'm sure glad you showed me, though."

"I wouldn't have it any other way."

"Well, me either," said Elvis, and they all laughed.

Lisa smiled and gathered her pile of tissues. "I'm a little amazed that you were able to get him to listen to you. Many have not had success in that area." She shot her dad a smirk and stood up.

Elvis rolled his eyes and grinned.

The sun was setting, and Elvis ordered out for dinner. The three of them sat talking for hours while they ate, shared, and laughed. It was late into the night before Jenna left.

Throughout her new relationship with Elvis, as their friendship deepened, so did the concerns and curiosity Jenna had about the flashes in her head of things she knew she had not experienced. As the days and weeks rolled by, the visions of things became more frequent and more detailed. They were too real to be imagination or made up. She remembered sitting downstairs at Graceland, watching TV. Movies and blowing bubbles with what Jenna somehow instinctively knew were Elvis' grandchildren. Walking with him down to the gates to watch him sign autographs. Boarding his private jet with him and taking off. Throwing bits of paper back and forth with his security team, howling with laughter as full popcorn wars erupted. Flashes of herself crying and hugging a smiling Elvis as he handed her a "Paid in Full" receipt for college. Snowball fights. Cocoa. Standing with him at his parent's graves. Him standing with her at Nan's grave. Christmas and birthday gifts. Reading online about events he attended and she did not, and smiling at the good reviews. There were a few arguments as well, one with actual yelling and Elvis storming out of the house, but every time Jenna tried to grasp at what they argued over, details became elusive.

Hesitantly she broached this subject with Elvis, asking him questions to try to ascertain her own sanity. For weeks his answers were always vague, with a smile, and maybe a hug. Finally, after about a month and a half, Jenna could no longer separate what she knew before Elvis came to her and what she knew after. She tried to recall what Chris and Bill had told her about timelines, but the memories were muddy and vague. She needed answers, and somehow she absolutely knew he had them.

"Elvis, were you told anything about the universe righting itself after I got back?" Jenna asked, sitting on a bench beside him behind the house.

Elvis' head snapped up and he was immediately focused. "Righting itself?"

"Yeah. Okay. So, since I got back, I have been having more and more and more, like, visions, I guess?"

"Visions? What do you mean?"

"Yeah, like, flashes of stuff in my head is how they started out. But now they're like real memories and they seem to have replaced my old memories.

For example, I can't remember what the Jungle Room looked like. I can barely remember that it was ever even called that. All I can actually remember is how it looks now. Stuff like that. There are memories of you and me, and all kinds of stuff we did. But on some level it seems somehow like I'm supposed to think we didn't. Or did we? I'm getting worried about this. Worried that something got scrambled in the jumps." Jenna twisted her owl ring and felt self-conscious.

Elvis smiled gently and took her hand. "I've been waiting for you to get here." Jenna looked confused. "I have been careful about what I revealed because I wanted you to merge the two sets of memories yourself. If I forced it, I was afraid your head would explode or something." He chuckled and patted her hand. "But I see you've arrived."

Jenna shifted toward him and took his other hand. He looked at her, then gazed out toward the horses milling in the field.

"When I went to St. Louis to verify you'd been born, I found out you had been, obviously. I came home and decided to wait. I wanted to wait until you were grown and of age before I made an overture to bring you into my insane life. It was absolute torture to wait all that time without being able to see you. Waiting for you to grow up—to become the Jenna I had met all those years ago." He smiled and sighed. "So, in '06 when I played in St. Louis, I asked my guys to find you and make sure you'd been moved to the front row. I saw you, and waited till the right moment, then pulled you up onstage. Do you have memories of this yet?"

Jenna blinked and held her breath as a flood of images raced through her head. That green and white suit. He was holding her hand onstage in front of thousands of people. She was crying and shaking with adoration and excitement. He sang a song to her, he hugged her. Nan was sobbing in their seats. Now she was behind the drums. Backstage. Jenna gasped and her voice shook. Her hand went to her mouth and she struggled to process her thoughts.

"God, that really happened, didn't it? I've had flashes of that for a month. We didn't win some contest to move to the front. That was you? It all actually happened…"

"It did indeed. It was all I could do to keep from jumping right off the stage to see you again. And from that moment on, you were part of everything. You saved my life, and I love you like no other person on this earth." His eyes shone with genuine affection and love.

Jenna was utterly stunned. None of these "flashes" these last weeks were her going crazy. They happened. They really happened. She'd been a part of Elvis' life for 14 years and was only just now remembering it as the "old" path merged with the new one she created. He and Nan had also forged a friendship, and he included her in many activities. He attended and paid for Nan's funeral, and sent flowers to the gravesite every week.

Jenna was a regular visitor to Graceland. She came three or four times a week, and they grew closer than ever. They ate together, watched movies, laughed and teased. They strolled around Graceland, fed apples to the horses, and rode golf carts—though not at the dizzying speeds Elvis recounted from his younger years. Lisa came as regularly as her schedule would allow, and on several occasions, she brought Priscilla or her children with her. Jenna found Priscilla to be warm, gracious, and absolutely devoted to Lisa, Elvis, and her family. Jenna often drove him back to her apartment, and they sat together on the window bench again, laughing, sharing, and being together. At his request, she made him many more grilled cheese sandwiches and potato chips. She accompanied him in his jet to Los Angeles a few times for appearances, and once for a day in a recording booth doing a voice recording for a PSA. She kept amusedly silent while Elvis assured the press again and again that Jenna was not his girlfriend or secret, hidden daughter. She sat quietly in the den at Graceland, marveling at the impressive recording studio that was set up as Elvis recorded three songs for an upcoming soundtrack. He came to an awed, standing-room-only crowd for two semesters to speak to her students about the dawning of rock and roll. There was stunned silence when her classes all realized she actually knew Elvis Presley. Her classes had to be moved on those days to huge lecture halls to satisfy the demand of starry-eyed students and faculty alike. Elvis affably sat on a comfy chair on the stage, his cane resting on the arm of the chair, patiently answering questions while his security detail watched from backstage.

Later that year, Elvis' health began to decline, and his heart wasn't working very well anymore. He insisted on their walks around Graceland's grounds every week, always wearing one of his many hats at a jaunty angle, but now he was often in a wheelchair that Jenna pushed. She knew her time with him was running short and she hated it with her whole soul. He'd been tiring out much more easily and often seemed more out of breath. His full-time nurses kept oxygen for him to use, but it wasn't helping for long. He completed a voice recording on Sunday, and by the end of that week, she wasn't sure he could have done it. He was rapidly deteriorating and her heart ached at the idea of losing him. Lisa and her children arrived that week for an extended stay.

Elvis died on Saturday, November 12, 2022, peacefully, at the age of 87. Jenna was called to the house but was unable to arrive before he passed away as he slept. Lisa and her children were with him, and Priscilla was on a flight bound for Memphis within an hour. Lisa pulled Jenna aside and gave her a shoe-box sized wooden box, sealed with tape. She explained her father had directed her to get it out of a closet, and make sure it was delivered if he died before Jenna got there. Jenna clutched the box and sat down across the hall in his office. Tape broken, she saw dozens and dozens of pictures. Pictures of Jenna, Elvis, Lisa, Lisa's kids, Nan... Fourteen years of pictures of a deep friendship after time's ripples and realities merged into one, and the seams of those ripples were sealed. He'd written on the back of many of them—dates, times, places, little comments, silly little drawings. She would go through each one as though it were a precious jewel. Lying on the top of the pictures was Elvis' "improved" owl pendant. Jenna held it to her heart and cried.

His recorded version of "I Will Always Love You" from 1974 was played as thousands upon thousands of people attended the huge outdoor funeral in Memphis, honoring the almost 70-year career of the most famous man who ever lived. Odd looks were exchanged but no questions were asked when Lisa and Priscilla insisted that two strangers named Bill and Chris be seated with Jenna and the family. Elvis had worked until the week he died, and Jenna knew he wouldn't want it any other way. His reclamation was complete—his purpose fulfilled. The tens of thousands who came to mourn his passing stood side by side—black and white, rich and poor, liberal and conservative. They stood shoulder to shoulder from every country, every state, every walk of life, united in their love and respect for this man. His decades-spanning influence was so deeply profound, so incredibly widespread that there were no barriers to whom he touched. Elvis had, in fact, changed the world. The world, in turn, gathered to respect and mourn a life well-lived. Jenna mourned her dear friend.

Printed in Great Britain
by Amazon

30781616R00075